# DEATH LEAVES
# NO CARD

# DEATH LEAVES NO CARD

by

## Miles Burton

RAMBLE HOUSE

ISBN 13: 978-1-60543-348-6

ISBN 10: 1-60543-348-9

Cover Art: Gavin L. O'Keefe
Preparation: Fender Tucker

*CHAPTER ONE*

R EUBEN DUKES worked his crowbar into the door and its frame and gave it a sharp wrench. As the door flew open revealing the interior of the bathroom, there was an instant's silence, broken by a shrill scream from Hetty Dukes and a deeper "Mercy on us!" from her mother.

Reuben strode into the room, snatched a bath towel from the rail and flung it over the naked figure. Then he turned to the two women standing petrified upon the landing.

"Down into the kitchen, both of you," he growled in a deep voice. "Your master and I can manage this job. We'll call you if we want you."

He waited until his wife and daughter had clattered downstairs, then looked searchingly at his master. From the very first, from that moment ten minutes ago, he had a vague suspicion that something queer had happened. Hetty had come dashing breathlessly into the cowshed with the amazing story that Mr. Basil had fainted in the bathroom and that they couldn't get the door open. Fainted! Mr. Basil had merely fainted by the look of him. But in *his* master's dim, short-sighted eyes he could read nothing but helpless bewilderment.

Mr. Geoffrey Maplewood was not looking his best. He was wearing fur-lined bedroom slippers and a purple silk dressing-gown under which were a pair of pale green pyjamas. He had not yet shaved, and a dark shadow covered his thin, pallid cheeks and receding chin. His black hair, usually so carefully groomed, was in disorder and hung in ridiculous wisps over his high forehead. Meeting his bailiff's steady glance, he opened his mouth to speak, then shut it again irresolutely.

Reuben shook his head slowly, indicating that it was a bad business, whichever way one looked at it.

"Best send for the doctor straight away, sir," he said brusquely.

Mr. Geoffrey Maplewood suddenly found his voice. "Yes, yes. the doctor, of course," he gabbled. "Dear me, I can't remember his name. I hardly know him. I can't understand it. Basil's always been so extraordinarily healthy. I've never known anything like this to happen before."

But Reuben was not listening to him. He had crossed the passage to the head of the stairs and was leaning over the banister. "Hetty?" he called.

His daughter could not have been far away, for she answered him immediately. "Yes, Dad."

"Run along to the farm and ring up Dr. Prescott. Tell him that Mr. Maplewood's nephew has been taken bad suddenly, and ask him to come along as soon as he can. Hurry, now."

A door slammed as Hetty sped on her errand. Reuben turned towards the bathroom and stood staring gloomily at the motionless figure, of which only the head and shoulders were now visible, protruding from the decent shrouding of the towel.

"We'd best get Mr. Basil into his room before the doctor comes, sir," he said. "He's awkward lying there like that, as he is."

"Yes, yes, certainly," Mr. Maplewood agreed mechanically. "Into his room, of course, the farther one at the end of the passage. Do you think we can carry him between us, Dukes?"

"You leave that to me, sir," Reuben replied. By general consent he was the strongest man at Tenteridge, or for many miles round. He entered the bathroom and with an apologetic gesture removed the towel. He had been quite right when he said Basil Maplewood was awkward where he was, for that young man was lying in an extraordinary position. His body was on its right side on the bathroom floor, with the right leg drawn up closely against it. His left leg hung over the bath so that the inner side of the knee rested upon the porcelain rim, and the foot and ankle dangled in the water.

With one arm under both thighs and the other supporting the small of the back, Reuben lifted his burden with scarcely an effort. He carried Basil Maplewood to his room and laid him gently on the bed, drawing the sheet over him for the sake of decency. Then he left the room, closing the door quietly but determinedly behind him. Mr. Geoffrey Maplewood was not to be seen. He had presumably retired to his own bedroom, for the door of this was now shut. Reuben, after a further glance through the open door of the bathroom, went downstairs and joined his wife in the kitchen.

Emily Dukes looked up eagerly as he came in. "Oh, there you are, then!" she exclaimed. "Whatever have you been doing? Isn't there anything I can do for the poor young gentleman?"

Reuben shook his head slowly. "There's nothing you can do, no, nor the doctor either," he replied. "Trust me to know a dead man when I see him."

"Dead!" Mrs. Dukes exclaimed shrilly. "Why, how can that be? Mr. Basil was as well as could be not half an hour ago."

Reuben raised a warning hand. "Not so loud, Mother," he replied. "There's so need to make a fuss. It's no affair of ours if Mr. Basil's dead. It's for the master to explain how it happened. And the less you or I know about it, the better."

But Mrs. Dukes was not to be silenced. "It's all very well for you to talk like that," he said; "but they'll be asking questions of us, as you know well enough. And when I took Mr. Basil his cup of tea, he was as spry as I've ever seen him."

Reuben shrugged his shoulders. "That's as may be," he said. "He's none so spry now. What's become of that girl? It's time she was back here by now."

"That'll be her," replied Mrs. Dukes as light footsteps became audible outside the back door. And a moment later Hetty, breathless and attractive, burst into the kitchen.

"I spoke to the doctor himself," she announced. "He says he'll get out his car at once and be round here inside ten minutes."

Her mother glanced at the clock. "Just after nine," she remarked. "Being Sunday morning, the doctor hasn't got his surgery till ten."

Reuben snorted. "Surgery!" he exclaimed. "There's something more for him to do upstairs than daub iodine on sprained wrists." He stopped abruptly, catching a warning glance from his wife.

But the significance of his tone had not been lost on Hetty. "Why, is the young gentleman as bad as all that?" she asked.

"How should I know, child?" her father replied gruffly. "It's for the doctor to say how bad he is. What else is he coming for?"

Silence fell upon the kitchen, broken only by the sounds of Mrs. Dukes's rather aimless pottering over the gas stove. She hardly knew what to be getting on with, since it seemed now that that breakfast she had been preparing would never be eaten. Such a shame, for she'd gone to a lot of trouble. Dried haddock stewed in milk with sausages and bacon to follow. With an air of resignation she took the sizzling frying-pan off the stove and laid it on the table.

The kitchen clock ticked its way deliberately through the minutes, until at last Reuben's straining ears caught the sound of an approaching car. "There's the doctor," he exclaimed. "Run and open the front door, Hetty, there's a good girl."

The car drew up at the gate and a few seconds later Dr. Prescott appeared at the front door, bag in hand. He was a youngish man, small and wiry, with an alert look in his stern gray eyes. "Here I am, Miss Dukes," he said briskly. "Where's the patient?"

At the sound of his voice Reuben had entered the hall from the kitchen. "I'll show you if you come this way, Doctor," he replied.

"Hallo, you here, Dukes!" exclaimed the doctor in some astonishment. "All right, lead the way, I'll follow."

As they mounted the stairs, a bedroom door opened and Mr. Geoffrey Maplewood appeared. He had been dressing, but had not completed the operation, for he was in his shirt sleeves, unshaven and with hair unbrushed. But he had put on his glasses and recognised the doctor.

"Oh, good morning," he said. "I'm so glad you've come, Doctor—"

The doctor finished his sentence for him. "Prescott," he remarked crisply. "I hear your nephew has been taken ill, Mr. Maplewood."

"Yes, a most extraordinary thing. Fainted in the bathroom. I've never known such a thing to happen to him before. And with the door locked, too. We had to send for Dukes. If it hadn't been for him, I don't know how we should have got into the room."

Dr. Prescott nodded a trifle impatiently. "Yes, yes, you can tell me about that later. I had better see your nephew first."

Reuben put an end to the conversation. "This way, sir," he said. He walked along the passage and opened the door of the farthest bedroom. "In here, sir."

The doctor entered the room, closely followed by Reuben, who shut the door after them. Prescott approached the bed and drew back the sheet. For several seconds he stood there, silent and motionless, with a gathering frown upon his face. At last he swung round and faced Reuben with accusing eyes. "You knew that this man was dead?" he asked sharply.

Reuben's eyes met the doctor's unfalteringly. "I guessed as much, sir, when I carried him in here from the bathroom," he replied.

"All right, I shan't want you in here. Go and stand in the passage and see that nobody goes into the bathroom until I've had a chance of looking in there myself."

It was ten minutes or more before Prescott emerged from the room to find Reuben standing sentinel over the bathroom. The door of Mr. Geoffrey Maplewood's bedroom was once more shut and he could be heard moving about inside. The doctor listened for a moment and then addressed Reuben abruptly. "What was the dead man's name?"

"Mr. Basil Maplewood, sir," Reuben replied. "He was Mr. Maplewood's nephew, but he didn't come from these parts. He lived at a place called Hithering Court, which I believe is near Staplemouth."

"How long has he been staying here?"

"He only came over with Mr. Maplewood yesterday afternoon, sir."

"There's no electric light laid onto this house, is there?"

"No, sir. Mr. Maplewood put in calor gas a couple of years or so ago. Before then they used to use lamps."

"Telephone?"

"No, sir. Mr. Maplewood always uses the telephone down at the farm."

"Wireless?"

"No, sir. I've heard Mr. Maplewood say that he doesn't care for it."

"All right. From what I can make out, you carried the dead man out of the bathroom yourself. Is that so?"

"Yes, sir. Mr. Maplewood sent for me to break the door open, so I came along with my bar and—"

"Never mind all that for a moment. How was the dead man lying when you found him? Show me."

Reluctantly Reuben lowered himself to the floor and assumed the position in which he had found Basil Maplewood. "Just like that, sir," he said.

"With the left foot hanging over the edge of the bath?" Prescott inquired. "You're quite sure of that?"

"Perfectly certain, sir. Mr. Basil's left foot was actually in the water."

Prescott put his hand into the water, which was still warm and perfectly clear, with no trace of soap in it. He looked carefully round the room without, however, touching any of the objects it contained. While he was so engaged, Mr. Geoffrey Maplewood appeared. He had a razor and a towel in his hand and was evidently about to shave at the basin in the bathroom.

But Prescott barred the way. "I shouldn't go in there, if I were you, Mr. Maplewood," he said quietly. "In fact, I think it would be safer if everybody left the house until it has been properly examined. There's something here that isn't quite right, I'm afraid."

"Dear me, how very disturbing," Mr. Maplewood exclaimed. "But Basil, my nephew? You've managed to bring him round all right, I hope?"

The doctor looked Mr. Maplewood straight in the face. "Your nephew is dead, Mr. Maplewood," he said abruptly.

The razor clattered from Mr. Maplewood's hand onto the floor. "Dead!" he repeated uncomprehendingly. "Dead?" His eyes blinked rapidly behind his glasses under Prescott's steady gaze. "I can't believe it. Why, I heard him whistling as he went into the bathroom. What did he die of?"

"That is a matter for a coroner's jury to decide," the doctor replied quietly. "You understand, of course, Mr. Maplewood, that it is my duty to communicate with him. And, meanwhile, I should like to repeat my suggestion that everybody should leave the house immediately."

Mr. Maplewood recoiled nervously from the bathroom door. "Is there any danger?" he asked.

"It would appear that there is very considerable danger," Prescott replied dryly.

## CHAPTER TWO

IT WAS JUST after two o'clock on the afternoon of Sunday, February 20th, that Inspector Arnold of Scotland Yard arrived at Addleford Police Station. He was immediately ushered into the presence of Superintendent Garland, who welcomed him with outstretched hand.

"You haven't wasted any time, Inspector," he said. "Sit down and make yourself comfortable. You'll find a box of cigarettes and some matches on that desk."

"Thanks very much," Arnold replied as he took the proffered seat. "But I'd rather smoke my pipe, if you don't mind."

"Just as you please. Now, you'll want to know what made us summon the Yard to our assistance. And I'll begin by warning you that the whole thing may turn out to be a mare's nest. By which I mean that, although there's undoubtedly a dead man in the case, there appears to be no evidence that a crime has been committed."

"Sounds interesting," Arnold commented. "Your dead man doesn't show any sign of having been murdered."

"You've got it exactly. I'll tell you what's happened as briefly as I can. We have here a citizen of credit and renown—Geoffrey Maplewood by name. He's a man getting on for fifty, unmarried, and lives with his sister in a fair-sized house called Riverbank. His household, I am told, consists of three indoor servants and a chauffeur.

"Mr. Maplewood is the owner of the Addle Paper Mill, which you may have noticed from the train just before you got to the station here. At one time he had a partner who got himself into serious trouble; but that's another story. Mr. Maplewood is now the sole owner of the mill and, by all accounts, does very well out of it.

"His hobby is farming. He owns Forsfel Farm at Tenteridge about twenty miles from here. But, of course, he doesn't run it himself. His business doesn't give him time for that. He has a bailiff, Dukes by name, who lives in the farmhouse. Some years ago Mr. Maplewood converted what used to be the bailiff's house to his own use. He put in a bathroom and a few other improvements like that, you understand. This house has no particular name.

Dukes speaks of it as 'the master's house,' and it has come to be known in the village as the master's house, or just simply the house.

"It is Mr. Maplewood's almost invariable habit to spend the week-ends there, leaving Riberbank directly after lunch on Saturday, and returning in time for Sunday's supper. While he's at the house, the bailiff's wife and daughter come up from the farm to do his cooking and that sort of thing. Usually, I am told, he spends his week-ends alone, but yesterday he took his nephew, Basil Maplewood, with him.

"Mind, I haven't yet made any detailed inquiries, and I can't tell you much about this nephew of his. All I can say is that he had no connection with this town. He had a place of his own somewhere near Staplemouth, which, as I dare say you know, is on the south coast rather more than a hundred miles from here. Any questions so far?"

Arnold looked up from his notebook in which he was jotting down the particulars given by the Superintendent. "No, I think not," he replied. "We have uncle and nephew established at the master's house. They spent last night there?"

"According to my information they did. Some time after eight o'clock this morning Basil, the nephew, went to the bathroom. He was there for what seemed an unreasonable time and his uncle, getting impatient, knocked on the door and told him to hurry up, or something like that. He couldn't get any answer, and came to the conclusion that Basil must have fainted. The door, a heavy, old-fashioned affair, was locked and he couldn't force it open. So the bailiff's daughter was sent down to the farm to fetch her father.

"Dukes arrived on the scene with a crowbar and very soon forced the door open. There was Basil right enough, lying on the floor stark naked, with one foot hanging over the edge of the bath. Dukes picked him up, carried him to his bedroom and the doctor was sent for. But Dukes, apparently, had already formed a pretty shrewd idea that he was carrying a dead body."

"Pity he didn't leave it alone then," said Arnold. "Did anyone else see how the body was lying?"

"Three other people. Mr. Maplewood, Mrs. Dukes and her daughter. It must have been a pretty severe shock to the ladies' modesty, I imagine. Well, the doctor came and examined the body. He's a youngish chap by name Prescott, and he hasn't been in practice in Tenteridge very long. But he's got his head screwed on the right way, and he took charge of the situation.

"I'm not going to repeat what he told me. You'd better by far hear it in his own words. The long and short of it is that he wasn't a bit satisfied as to the cause of death. On the face of it, there was nothing whatever to account for Basil's conking out so suddenly. So he did the best possible thing under the circumstances: He cleared every one out of the house, locked it up behind them and gave the keys to the local constable. Then he rang me up and gave it as his opinion that there was something very queer about the whole business."

"Did he suggest that Basil Maplewood had been murdered?" Arnold asked.

"No, he didn't do that exactly; but he said that he found it very difficult to believe that he had died from natural causes. The Coroner had been notified and, at Prescott's suggestion, has asked for a pathologist from the Home Office to perform the postmortem. He's coming down tomorrow morning. As I said before, he may discover that the whole thing is a mare's nest. But, in case he doesn't the chief constable and I are agreed that it would be just as well to have the Yard on the spot.

"Now I want you to feel perfectly free to take what steps you like. I've got a car at your disposal and a driver who knows the district perfectly. Mr. Maplewood is at Riverbank, and he has assured me that he won't leave there without letting me know. Dr. Prescott lives at the village of Tenteridge and will be in, barring unexpected calls, all the afternoon. Dukes and his family are at Forstal Farm. The local constable, whose name is Terry, is prowling round the master's house with the keys in his pocket."

Arnold smiled. "You've made everything as easy as possible for me, and I'm sure I'm deeply grateful," he said. "I'd better have a chat with the doctor first and then look over the house."

"Very well, the car's outside and the driver's waiting. His name's Lambert, and you'll find him a very decent chap. Let me know how you get on, and if there's anything I can do to help, you've only got to ask."

The car proved capable of a very creditable turn of speed, and under the skilled direction of Lambert they reached Tenteridge in something over half an hour. In the course of conversation, Arnold discovered that Lambert was a native of Tenteridge, where his parents still kept a general shop and post office. Also, it transpired that he knew the Dukes family well, though for some reason he seemed reluctant to talk about them. Of Mr. Geoffrey Maplewood he knew little or nothing except that Dukes always seemed to get on well enough with him.

Dr. Prescott lived in a substantial red brick house standing in the centre of the village. The door was opened by a tall, graceful woman who told Arnold that she was Mrs. Prescott, and that her husband would see him at once in the consulting room. On entering this sanctum, Arnold found the doctor seated at his desk making entries in his case-book.

"Sit down, Inspector," he said cordially. "I was expecting you, for Garland rang up just now to say that you were on your way. Ask me any questions you like and I'll do my best to answer them."

"Thank you, Doctor," Arnold replied. "Perhaps, to begin with, you will tell me how you were called to the master's house this morning?"

"Certainly. While I was having breakfast this morning the telephone bell rang. I answered the call and spoke to Hetty Dukes, who told me that she was ringing up from the farm. She said that Mr. Maplewood's nephew had been taken bad and asked me to go to the master's house at once. I promised to do so, and made a note of the time of the call. It was then ten minutes past nine."

"I had better make it quite plain that I am not and never have been Mr. Maplewood's medical attendant. My acquaintance with him is of the slightest, and I do not suppose that before this morning I have spoken to him more than two or three times. As for his nephew, I was not even aware that such a person existed.

"On arriving at the house, I was shown into what I understand is the spare bedroom. Lying on the bed there was the naked body of a young man covered only by a sheet. Dukes told me that he had himself carried the body from the bathroom. It was twenty-three minutes past nine when I examined the body and came to the conclusion that death had taken place less than an hour previously."

"Thank you, Doctor, that's perfectly clear," said Arnold. "Do I understand that you were unable to satisfy yourself as to the cause of death?"

"Let me answer that question at some length. I examined the body very carefully for signs of external injuries. I found slight bruising on the right hip, the point of the right shoulder and the right side of the head in the region of the temple. These bruises were quite recent and might have been inflicted either just before or just after death. I am told that the deceased was found lying on his right side. In my opinion, the bruises might have been caused by deceased falling on the floor, from an erect or semi-erect position.

"These bruises were the only signs of external injury that I could find. If any internal injuries exist, the post-mortem will of course reveal them. The appearance of the body is that of a young man, physically fit and perfectly healthy. I do not think that there is any likelihood of his having suffered from any disease which would render him liable to sudden collapse. And yet it would appear that he was in the act of getting into his bath when he fell to the floor. I shall be very greatly surprised if the post-mortem discloses that death was due to natural causes."

"Have you any suspicion how this young man may have been killed?" Arnold asked.

Prescott shook his head. "I have not," he replied. "Once, during my hospital days, I had the opportunity to examine the body of a man who had been killed by accidentally touching a high-tension electric cable. In this case there were no signs whatever of external or internal injuries. Now, as you are doubtless aware, fatal results have been caused by defective electrical fittings in bathrooms, the reason being that wet skin is a better conductor than dry.

"But in this case there is no possibility of death having been caused by an electric shock. Current from the grid is laid onto the village itself at the standard pressure of 230 volts. But this supply does not extend to Forstal Farm or the house. There is, I believe, a private plant at the farm, but this supplies the surrounding buildings only and not the house. There is no telephone in the house or even a wireless set. In fact, it appears to be one of the very few houses nowadays which contain no electrical apparatus at all, not even a doorbell."

"It was quite fine in London between eight and nine o'clock this morning," Arnold remarked.

"So it was here. Besides, lightning doesn't strike a person in a closed room without leaving some trace of its passage. Now I'll be perfectly frank with you, Inspector. I do not know how Basil Maplewood died, and I very much doubt whether the postmortem will enlighten us. Under these circumstances, I felt it my duty to report the matter not only to the coroner, but to the Superintendent as well."

"You were perfectly right, Doctor," said Arnold. "I needn't trouble you any more now. I'm just going to look over the house for myself."

"I'll come with you if you like," Prescott replied. "I'm not particularly busy this afternoon."

Arnold accepted this offer gratefully, and they set out. Leaving the village at the farther end, they followed a country road for rather less than a mile, passing nothing but half a dozen scattered cottages. At the end of two or three minutes Lambert pulled up at a gateway set in a low garden wall.

Behind the wall was a shrubbery of evergreens, roughly trimmed, and about ten yards deep. Beyond this stood a small house, brick built with a tiled roof. As Arnold and Prescott got out of the car, a policeman in uniform appeared at the gate and, recognizing the doctor, saluted rather carelessly.

"Hallo, Terry," said Prescott. "Still on duty, then? This is Inspector Arnold from Scotland Yard who has come to look over the house."

Terry sprang smartly to attention and saluted again, this time with military precision.

"You have the key, I understand?" said Arnold as he returned the salute.

The policeman's hand dived into his pocket. "Here it is, sir?" he replied.

Arnold took the key. "I'd like to look round the outside first if it won't waste your time, Doctor," he said.

Dr. Prescott raised no objection, and together they explored the exterior of the house. They found that it had two entrances, a front door with a porch on the south side and a back door without a porch on the north side. From each of these doors a narrow path ran through the shrubbery to a corresponding gate in the low wall which separated the property from the road. These paths were gravelled and in quite good condition. The shrubbery occupied the whole of the space between the eastern front of the house and the low wall.

Following the path past the front porch, they reached the western side of the house. Here they found a small ornamental lawn with a herbaceous border at its farther side. A chestnut fence divided the border from an extensive and closely planted apple orchard.

"Just the place for a quiet weekend," Prescott remarked. "Mr. Geoffrey Maplewood only spends Saturday and Sunday here, I gather. Shall we have a look inside?"

Arnold unlocked the front door and they walked into a miniature hall. Three doors opened off this. The first on the right of the front door led into a dining-room, of which the single window looked out into the shrubbery. The second door nearly opposite the first led into a big cheerful room furnished as a lounge. The two windows of this room looked out over the lawn towards the orchard.

The third door at the farther end of the hall from the front door was covered with baize and closed with a spring. Pushing this open, they found themselves in the kitchen, the single window of which looked out over the lawn. Adjoining the kitchen was the scullery which had a window looking into the shrubbery and into which the back door opened. A larder, coal cellar and outside lavatory completed the back premises.

A short flight of stairs ran from the hall onto a landing above. On this floor there were two bedrooms, one over the lounge and the other over the kitchen. What had originally been a third bedroom over the dining-room had been divided by a partition into two parts. The larger part formed the bathroom, the smaller the lavatory. There was yet another room over the scullery, quite small and used as a boxroom.

The house was in a state of considerable disorder. Fires had been lighted in the lounge and dining-room, but these had burnt out and the ashes were only warm. In the dining-room the table was laid for breakfast, and a rack of toast stood on it. The kitchen table was covered with culinary utensils, a stew-pan and a kettle stood on the gas stove, and a row of plates in the rack. In the scullery the anthracite boiler, though still alight, had burnt very low.

Prescott pointed these things out to Arnold with a touch of pardonable pride. "I cleared them all out without giving them a chance to tidy anything up," he said. "I wanted the police to see the place exactly as it was when I was called in. And when they'd all gone I had a look round to satisfy myself. I saw that all the windows and doors were shut and fastened and the back door locked with the key on the inside and bolted. Then I went out, locked the front door behind me and gave the key to Terry. I can see that nobody has been inside the place since then."

"It'll be the greatest help to us, I'm sure," said Arnold vaguely. "The body is still here, I suppose?"

"That won't have moved far," Prescott replied. "Come along upstairs and I'll show it to you."

They entered the bedroom above the kitchen. The body of Basil Maplewood lay on the bed as Reuben had placed it that morning.

Prescott drew back the sheet, exposing a handsome young face with fair hair and clear-cut features.

"You can see the bruises for yourself," said the doctor, pointing them out one by one. "They're naturally more distinct than they were this morning. But as you can see they are all quite trivial. And the more I look at the body, the more convinced I become that we shall find no trace of organic disease tomorrow."

As the doctor replaced the sheet, Arnold looked about the room, which was plainly but adequately furnished. On the dressing-table was a pair of silver-backed hair-brushes, each engraved with the monogram B.R.M. A brown tweed suit and the appropriate underclothing lay folded on a chair at the foot of the bed. On another chair stood a leather suitcase, also bearing the initials B.R.M. Opening this, Arnold found that it held a dinner-jacket suit and various other garments of masculine attire.

Arnold felt in the breast pocket of the coat folded on the chair and produced a wallet. The contents of this were as follows: Notes to the amount of seventeen pounds; a few visiting cards bearing the name Mr. Basil R. Maplewood; a driving licence issued by the Hampshire County Council to Basil Robert Maplewood, Esq., of Hithering Court, near Staplemouth; an insurance certificate in the same name covering a car DKR163; the return halves of two first-class railway tickets, the first issued on February 17th, available for the return journey from Waterloo to Staplemouth. The second issued on February 9th, from Addleford to Victoria.

"We'd better have a look at the bathroom," said Prescott as Arnold returned the wallet to the pocket. "It was there, by all accounts, that the poor young fellow died. If what I'm told is correct, he was in the act of getting into his bath when it happened."

The bathroom had evidently been equipped by the local plumber, efficiently enough, but without any attempt at elaboration. The floor was covered with rubber sheeting, not too accurately fitted. The walls had been tiled rather unevenly to a height of four feet from the floor. At one side of the room stood a plain porcelain-finished bath, and at the other a lavatory basin. Hot and cold water pipes had been led to each of these, terminating in plain brass taps over but not fitted to them. Above the basin was a plain mirror and a wooden shelf enameled white. The single casement window, which was shut and fastened, was glazed with ordinary ground glass.

Arnold pointed to this. "Do you know if the window was like that when the body was found, Doctor?" he asked.

"I can't say," Prescott replied. "But when I came in here this morning it was open on the first peg. I shut it when I looked round the house after I'd seen the folks safely out of it."

Arnold next turned his attention to the door. The application of Reuben's crowbar had torn the hasp clean off the doorpost without injuring the lock itself. The bolt was still protruding and the key was in place on the inside of the door. Arnold tried it and found that it turned easily enough.

Hanging on hooks screwed to the inner side of the door were a highly spectacular dressing-gown of silk and a pair of pyjamas, also silk, yellow with blue trimmings. A pair of bedroom slippers lay on the floor beside the bath. On the wooden shelf there was a safety razor taken to pieces, a stick of shaving soap with the lid off the box and a shaving brush still damp. On a wooden horse were a face-towel showing signs of use and a bath towel unused and still folded as it had come from the laundry. On a tray over the bath was a sponge quite dry, and a new cake of soap.

Prescott smiled as Arnold examined these objects in turn. "The story seems pretty clear up to a point, doesn't it?" he suggested.

"Looks like it," Arnold replied. "I noticed just now that Basil Maplewood's face was shaved, and that shaving gear on the shelf no doubt belonged to him. He brought it in here with him and locked the door. He turned on the bathwater and shaved at the basin while the bath was filling. But he never got so far as actually washing himself in the bath. The state of the water, to say nothing of the sponge and soap, shows that clearly enough."

Prescott nodded. "You'll hear what Dukes has to say about the position of the body when he found it. From his account it would seem that Basil was just stepping into the bath when he was killed. But how on earth did it happen? That's what I want to know."

"Perhaps the post-mortem will answer that question," Arnold replied. "I'd like to have a look round the other bedroom while I'm here."

Mr. Geoffrey Maplewood's room showed the same disorder as the rest of the house. The bed was unmade and a purple dressing-gown and a pair of green pyjamas had been flung across it. A number of toilet articles were scattered over the dressing-table. An inspection of the chest of drawers suggested that Mr. Maplewood kept a stock of clothing at the house for use during his week-end visits.

Arnold glanced at his watch. It was by now half-past four, and he still had plenty to do. "I've seen enough for the present," he said. "Do you know what arrangements have been made for the postmortem tomorrow?"

"Yes. The pathologist is coming down to Addleford tomorrow and Garland's going to drive him over here to meet me. As soon as he arrives we shall get on with the job. I've arranged with Dukes for him to bring up a trestle tabletop. We can put that on the bed in the spare room. Now, is there anything else I can do for you?"

"I think not, thanks very much, Doctor," Arnold replied. "I'm going along to the farm to see Dukes."

"You'll come to the farm about a quarter of a mile along the road. You can't miss it, for it's the first building you see on your left. I wonder if I might borrow your car to take me home."

They left the house together, locking the front door and returning the key to Terry. Lambert was instructed to drive the doctor back to the village and then bring the car to Forstal Farm. Then Arnold set off on foot in the opposite direction, towards the cluster of roofs which had been pointed out to him.

## CHAPTER THREE

HERE WAS A certain amount of traffic on the road that Sunday afternoon. Not enough to make walking along it unpleasant, but sufficient to show that it was to some extent a thoroughfare, but not a main one. A few cyclists, an occasional car and a single bus. During the five minutes which it took Arnold to reach Forstal Farm, he counted a round dozen vehicles in all.

The farm lay well back from the road, with a wide space in front of it from which it probably derived its name. Arnold walked across this yard and rapped on the farmhouse door, which was opened by a pleasant-faced woman whom he guessed to be Mrs. Dukes.

"My name is Arnold, and I've come from Scotland Yard," he said. "May I come in?"

"Oh, yes, of course, sir," Mrs. Dukes replied. "If you don't mind waiting a moment I'll fetch my husband."

Arnold entered the oak-beamed hall and a moment later Reuben appeared, wiping his mouth. "You want to see me, sir?" he asked. "It's about that terrible affair up at the house this morning, I dare say?"

Arnold nodded. "That's right," he replied. "I want you to tell me all you know about it."

"I'll do that with pleasure, sir, though it's little enough I know about it." Reuben hesitated for a moment, then continued: "We're just having a cup of tea in the kitchen, sir. If I might make so bold as to offer you a cup, I could bring it to you in the front room."

"A cup of tea!" Arnold exclaimed. "Just the very thing I've been longing for; but if it wouldn't be intruding, I'd rather have it in the kitchen with you all."

"It won't be any intrusion, sir," Reuben replied readily. "We're always ready for company on Sunday afternoon, though there doesn't happen to be any to-day. Come along and be sure of your welcome."

They went into the kitchen together and Arnold cast an admiring glance at the glowing range and the array of copper pans upon the dresser. Two women were standing by the laden table and Reuben nodded towards them.

"My wife—you met her when she opened the door to you just now," he said. "And that's my daughter, Hetty. Sit down, Inspector. Over this side by the fire. You'll find it warmer."

Arnold sat down in the high-backed wooden chair and Mrs. Dukes poured him out a cup of tea from a gigantic brown teapot. Then the three of them sat fidgeting uncomfortably and eyeing their guest with unconcealed awe.

Arnold hastened to break the silence. "I haven't had a real farmhouse tea like this for ages," he said. "I'm sure you won't mind if I start asking questions while I eat it. They'll be about Mr. Basil Maplewood, of course. To begin with, did he often stay with his uncle at the house?"

"Only once before, to the best of my recollection," Reuben replied. "That's right, isn't it, Mother?"

"Yes, that's right," Mrs. Dukes agreed. "It was some time last August, for I remember we'd just done picking the Beauty of Bath."

"Does Mr. Geoffrey Maplewood often bring visitors to the house for the week-end?"

"Scarcely ever these days," Reuben replied. "He nearly always comes over alone. I can't think of anybody except Mr. Basil who's been there for the last two years or more."

"There was Miss Monica last September," Hetty put in. "Don't you remember, Dad?" she went on. "She was here on the Sunday of the Harvest Festival."

"Quite right, child," said Reuben. "Miss Monica is Mr. Geoffrey's sister. But, apart from her and Mr. Basil, there've been no visitors to the house, since"—he hesitated and corrected himself—"for these last five years."

"Were visitors more frequent five years ago?" Arnold asked blandly.

Reuben and his wife exchanged glances. "Mr. Pelling used to come over pretty often at one time," the former replied slowly.

"Who is Mr. Pelling?"

Again that exchange of glances and a marked pause before Reuben replied.

"Mr. Pelling was Mr. Geoffrey Maplewood's partner. In the mill, you understand. But I'd rather you talked about Mr. Pelling to Mr. Geoffrey himself, sir."

Arnold remembered that Garland had said something about a partner who had got into trouble. For some reason the Dukes did not want to discuss the subject. It didn't matter, for Garland could supply any necessary information.

"What time did Mr. Maplewood and his nephew get to the house yesterday?" he asked.

"They came along here to the farm first," Reuben replied. "It was like this: Mr. Maplewood rang me from his office on Friday morning. He said that he was coming over as usual next day and that he'd want the spare room got ready, as he would be bringing Mr. Basil with him. And he said that Mr. Basil wanted to see the new disc harrow at work, and would I arrange to show it to him on Saturday afternoon.

"Well, the car came along here round about three yesterday afternoon, or maybe a few minutes later. The two gentlemen got out and Saxby—that's the chauffeur—drove back to the house to leave Mr. Basil's suitcase. I got the harrow and the tractor out in the near orchard, and the three of us went there together. I showed Mr. Basil how it worked myself, for I didn't want to have to turn out one of the chaps on Saturday afternoon. I dare say we were out in the orchard there getting on for an hour. Then the two gentlemen walked back to the house; and that's the last I saw of either of them until this morning."

Mrs. Dukes took up the tale. "I was waiting for them with the kettle boiling. I'd been at the house the best part of the day getting the beds made and seeing to the fires and that. Alf Saxby had left the suitcase and I'd taken it up to the spare bedroom. It was round about half-past four when the gentlemen came in. I made them their tea and then started getting things ready for their dinner. And soon after six Hetty came along and gave me a hand."

"One minute," said Arnold. "I noticed that there was no garage at the house. What became of Saxby and the car?"

"Saxby took it back to Addleford," Reuben replied. "He usually does that in case Miss Monica wants to use it. Now and again he stays here overnight and puts the car in the cart shed here, though that doesn't often happen. He was to have come and fetched the gentleman at three o'clock this afternoon."

"I see. Did either Mr. Maplewood or his nephew leave the house again yesterday evening after tea?"

"Not so far as I know," Mrs. Dukes replied. "They sat talking in the house all the time from tea to dinner. I served up at half-past seven sharp. Tomato soup, roast chicken and roes on toast to finish up with. Mr. Geoffrey doesn't ever eat very much, but Mr. Basil had a wonderful appetite."

"There was nothing left of the chicken but one leg when I brought it out of the dining-room," Hetty remarked.

"They went back into the lounge when they had finished their dinner," Mrs. Dukes continued. "That must have been a quarter-past eight, or thereabouts. By the time Hetty and I had finished washing up and tidying round, it was a few minutes past nine. I went into the lounge where the gentlemen were, and asked if there was anything more wanted, as I always do. Mr. Geoffrey said, 'No,' so I said good night, and Hetty and I came back home."

"Did you lock up the house when you left?" Arnold asked.

"Not the front door. But I locked the back door and took the key with me, so that I could get in in the morning."

"I want you to tell me about the keys. Who has them during the week when the house is empty?"

"I always keep the key of the back door. Either Hetty or I go along there every day to keep the place aired. We light a fire in the lounge one day, in the dining-room the next, and the boiler in the scullery is always kept going. It keeps the house nice and dry."

"And the front door key? Does Mr. Maplewood take that?"

Mrs. Dukes shook her head. "No, he never takes either of the keys. There's no occasion for him to. He always rings up and tells Reuben about when he's coming and one or other of us is at the house waiting for him."

"And when he leaves?"

"It's the same then. Either Hetty is there or I am, and when he's gone we lock and bolt the door and leave the key on the inside. Then we come out by the back door, lock it and take the key with us."

"What about the windows? Are they always kept shut when there's nobody in the house?"

"Shut and fastened," Mrs. Dukes replied emphatically. "I'm always very particular to see to that. I'm sure there's nobody in the village who'd think of touching anything. But if any of them kid-dies came along and saw a window open, as likely as not they'd slip in and pinch something. I always goes round the house before I leave and see that all the windows are fastened; and Hetty will tell you the same."

Hetty nodded. "That's right," she said. "If Mother doesn't go round, I do." She suddenly started as a faint rat-a-tap-tap came from a distant door. Then with a murmured apology she hurried from the room. Her parents paid no attention to her departure.

Arnold continued his inquiries. " Now we'll come to this morning," she said. "What time did you get to the house, Mrs. Dukes?"

"Hetty and I left here just before half-past seven," she replied. "It doesn't take us five minutes to get there. We unlocked the back door and set to work as usual. Hetty drew the curtains and lit the fire in the lounge and dining-room while I saw to the boiler and put a kettle on for the early tea.

"Mr. Maplewood is always very regular in his habits when he is at the house on Sunday morning. He likes to be called with his cup of tea at eight, and has his breakfast at nine sharp. So when the kitchen clock showed eight o'clock, I poured out two cups of tea and took them upstairs. I knocked at Mr. Geoffrey's door and he answered at once. So I went in and put his tea beside him."

"He was in bed, I suppose?"

"Oh, yes, he was in bed. As I drew back the curtains he asked me to tell Mr. Basil when I took in his tea that he could use the bathroom first. You see, there are no washing-stands in the bedrooms, only the basin in the bathroom."

"Yes, I noticed that for myself. Did Mr. Geoffrey say anything else to you?"

Mrs. Dukes shook her head. "No, he didn't," she replied. "I left his room and went along to Mr. Basil's. He must have been asleep, for I had to knock twice before he heard me. And when he did answer I went in with his tea and gave Mr. Geoffrey's message about the bathroom."

"Did he seem perfectly well as far as you could tell?"

"Perfectly. There wasn't the least thing the matter with him then. He sat up in bed and stretched himself, and then he said, 'All right, Mrs. Dukes. I'll slip along to the bathroom as soon as I've drunk my tea.' "

Arnold looked up as the door opened. But it was only Hetty, whose cheerful face seemed to have acquired a pinker hue during her absence. She slipped unostentatiously into her place and the conversation continued.

"What else did you do after you had called Mr. Basil?" Arnold asked.

"I picked up the gentleman's shoes, took them downstairs and gave them to Hetty. She took them to the scullery to clean them and I started getting the breakfast ready."

"Have you any idea what time it was then?"

"I looked at the kitchen clock to see how much time I'd got, and it said, ten minutes past eight. And it wasn't for another ten minutes that I heard the bathroom door slam and knew that Mr. Basil must have gone in there."

"You can hear the bathroom door from the kitchen?" Arnold asked.

"Not if the baize door's shut. But I'd got it hooked back, for Hetty was running backwards and forwards laying the table for breakfast."

"Let me see," said Arnold. "The bathroom is over the dining-room, isn't it? Did you hear anything when you were laying the table, Miss Dukes?"

"I wasn't taking any particular notice," Hetty replied. "But I did hear somebody go in there, and then I heard the water running into the bath. It was still running after I'd finished in the dining-room and gone into the lounge to do the dusting."

"You neither of you heard when the water stopped running, I suppose?"

Both women shook their heads, and Mrs. Dukes spoke: "We were both getting on with our work, and I don't suppose we were thinking about it."

"Let's see if we can get at it another way. When I looked at the bath just now it was about half full. You saw it this morning, Mr. Dukes. Do you agree with me?"

"Half full, or maybe a little more," Reuben replied.

"Have you any idea how long it takes to fill the bath to that depth?"

Mrs. Dukes considered this. "It's hard to say," she replied. "The water doesn't run very quickly. It's my belief that the pipes are getting furred up, for the water in these parts is terrible hard. Maybe it would take between five and ten minutes."

"Now I want you both to think very carefully," said Arnold impressively. "Did either of you hear anything else about that time?"

There were a few minutes of reflective silence before Hetty spoke. "I heard somebody whistling along the landing or in the bathroom. I never heard Mr. Geoffrey whistle, so it must have been Mr. Basil."

"Yes, I heard the whistling, too," Mrs. Dukes agreed. "It was about the time that I heard the bathroom door. Oh, yes, and there was that car standing in the road about the same time."

Arnold pricked up his ears. "A car standing in the road? I'd like to hear about that."

"I don't know that there's much to tell. While I was in the kitchen after I'd heard the bathroom door, I think it was, I happened to open the back door for something and heard a car standing in the road with the engine running. I thought it might be someone with something for one of the gentlemen, but nobody came to the door. So when Hetty came into the kitchen I told her to run out and see who it was."

"That's right," said Hetty. "I went along the back path to the gate, and it was only an old van. The driver had got out and was doing something to the engine. He seemed to be having some kind of trouble with it."

"Would you recognize him again if you saw him?"

Hetty shook her head. "I didn't see his face, for he'd got his head under the bonnet. All I could see was the dark coat he was wearing."

"Can you describe the van?"

"I didn't take particular notice of it. It was a shabby old thing not unlike the one the carrier's got. I came in and told mother it wasn't anyone for us, and I didn't think any more about it. The men must have got it going all right, for it wasn't there when I ran down to fetch dad."

"Do you remember which way it was heading?"

Hetty thought for a moment. "It was drawn up by the side of the road against the garden wall between the two gates. And it was pointing towards the village."

"Have either of you any idea of the time when the van was seen?"

"Well, it must have been before half-past eight," Mrs. Dukes replied. "I remember looking at the clock soon after Hetty had told me what it was, and it was just upon the half-hour then. And it wasn't long after that that I thought I heard something all upstairs, but I couldn't be sure of that. It might have been a door banging."

"I thought I heard something like that when I was in the lounge dusting," remarked Hetty. "And then everything seemed to be quiet about the house until Mr. Geoffrey started hammering on the bathroom door."

"That was ten to nine," Mrs. Dukes said. "I know that, for I'd just made the coffee and I always do that ten minutes before I serve breakfast. I couldn't make out what was happening, and I went into the hall to see. And then I heard Mr. Geoffrey call out, 'What's the matter, Basil? Are you all right? Why don't you answer me?'

"It seemed to me that something must be wrong, for Mr. Geoffrey to carry on like that. And after a bit he came to the top of the stairs and saw me. 'I can't make it out, Mrs. Dukes,' he said. "The bathroom door's locked and my nephew's inside, but I can't get him to answer.'

" 'Maybe the poor gentleman's fainted, sir,' I said, for I'd known things like that to happen before. 'I'll send my girl along to the farm to fetch Reuben. He'll soon get the door open.' And then Mr. Geoffrey said, 'I wish you would,' or something like that. Hetty had come into the hall, and she heard me talking. She heard what we said and ran off at once."

"I ran all the way home," said Hetty. "But it took me a minute or two to find dad. At last I found him in the cow shed at the back and told him what had happened."

"That's right," Reuben agreed. "She came along all out of breath and told me that Mr. Basil had fainted in his bath and nobody could open the door. So I went to the tool shed, got an iron bar and started off to the house. I happened to hear the grandfather clock in the passage strike nine as I left here. When I was three parts of the way to the house, Hetty overtook me on her bicycle. I told her to hurry on and tell her mother that I was coming."

Arnold turned to Mrs. Dukes. "What happened at the house while Miss Hetty was getting her father?" he asked.

"Mr. Geoffrey kept on knocking at the bathroom door, calling out Mr. Basil's name. Then he asked me if there was a ladder anywhere that we could put up outside the bathroom window and look in, and I told him that there wasn't one nearer than the farm. Then Hetty came back and said her dad was on the road, and a minute or so later he came in and went straight up to the bathroom."

Reuben followed with an account of his experiences, to which Arnold listened carefully.

"Well, that's all quite clear," he said. "I'd just like to ask a few more questions. When you first reached the house this morning you found the back door locked, of course."

"Yes, just as I'd left it the evening before."

"And the front door?"

Hetty replied to this: "When we heard the doctor's car coming, dad told me to go and open the front door. When I got to it it was locked and bolted with the key on the inside."

"And the windows? How were they?"

"They were all shut and fastened on the ground floor, weren't they, Hetty?"

"That's right," Hetty replied. "I noticed that in the lounge and dining-room when I drew back the curtains."

"How about the windows upstairs?"

"The landing window was shut and fastened," Mrs. Dukes replied. "Both Mr. Geoffrey and Mr. Basil had their windows a little way open when 1 called them. I can't say anything about the box-room or bathroom, for I didn't go into either."

"You're quite sure that when you reached the house there was nobody in it but the two gentlemen? It isn't possible that someone had got in during the night and was hiding there?"

Mrs. Dukes shook her head. "I don't see how anybody could have done that," she replied. "They could only have got in by one of the upper windows, which happened to be open. And they could never have done that without one of the gentlemen hearing."

This seemed logical enough as far as it went.

"Tell me what happened after you all left the house this morning," was Arnold's next question.

"It was the doctor who told us to go," Reuben replied. "He said it wasn't safe for anyone to stop in the house until it had been properly examined. So we came back here, Mr. Geoffrey came back with us, and terrible upset he was."

"He was that upset he hardly seemed to know what he was doing," Mrs. Dukes put in. "I asked him if he'd like me to get him some breakfast, as he hadn't had any. He just shook his head and didn't answer me. Then he started walking up and down the front room, picking things up and putting them back again, just as if he'd taken leave of his senses."

"I thought he'd be wanting to get back home," Reuben resumed. "So I rang up for Alf Saxby to come along with the car. I didn't say anything of what had happened, for it wasn't my business. The car came along round about a quarter to eleven, and Mr. Geoffrey went straight off in it."

"Did he say anything to any of you about his nephew's death before he went?"

They all shook their heads at this, and Reuben acted as spokesman. "He never said anything to anybody. It seemed as if he'd been knocked all of a heap."

"And you have heard nothing from him since then?"

"Not a word. As a matter of fact, we were wondering what we'd best do when you came along just now."

"I don't think there's very much you can do," Arnold replied.
"The house will be kept shut up for the present, and there's pretty
sure to be an inquest, which I expect you will all have to attend.
Well, I must thank you for a jolly good tea, Mrs. Dukes. Now I'll
be getting along."

He left the farm to find Lambert and the police car waiting in
the yard outside. "Have you been waiting here all the time I've
been inside?" he asked.

"I haven't been more than a few yards away, sir," Lambert replied.

"Then you must have seen who it was that went round to the
back door and knocked a little time ago."

Lambert flushed suddenly brick-red. "That was me, sir," he replied in confusion. "You see sir, me and Hetty—"

Arnold laughed. "Oh, I see. Well, good luck to you both. We'll
get back to Addleford now. But I want to stop and speak to Terry
on the way."

They found Terry, who had been relieved by one of his col-
leagues from the neighbouring village, having tea at his house in
Tenteridge. Arnold told him to make inquiries locally as to a
shabby-looking van said to have been standing outside the master's house round about half-past eight that morning, and then resumed his journey.

"Where would you like to go now, sir?" Lambert asked as they
reached the outskirt's of Addleford.

"I'd like to pay a call on Mr. Geoffrey Maplewood," Arnold
replied.

## CHAPTER FOUR

MR. MAPLEWOOD'S house, Riverbank, was appropriately named. It lay just outside the town of Addleford, on rising ground which sloped steeply down to the little River Addle. Below the house and almost half a mile down the river, farther on, where it flowed through the town, was a tall chimney which Lambert pointed out as that of the paper mill.

The car entered a drive gateway and, skirting the well-kept lawn, drew up at the front door. It was opened by an elderly maid in cap and apron who, in reply to Arnold's inquiry, informed him that Mr. Maplewood was at home. She showed him into a spacious drawing-room, containing a curious assortment of ancient and modern furniture. A woman seated at a bureau in the window jumped up hurriedly at the Inspector's entrance.

"Oh, good afternoon," she said warmly. "You want to see Geoffrey, of course. He's lying down, but Violet will call him. Isn't it terribly sad about poor Basil?"

As she turned to face him Arnold could only see her dimly as it was now after sunset and the lights in the room had not been switched on. He made out a medium-sized figure dressed in flowing black. Her features were indistinct, but Arnold was aware of a pair of sharp gray eyes behind heavy tortoise-shell glasses. He was searching for a fitting reply to her question when she forestalled him.

"I'm Basil's aunt, you know. Such a dear boy; always so good-natured and thoughtful. Geoffrey was so upset when he got back here this morning that it took me quite a long time to get him to tell me what had happened. And then, of course, I rang up Hithering Court and tried to get hold of poor little Phoebe. But she's gone to lunch with somebody in Staplemouth, and they couldn't tell me where to find her, so I had to leave a message. Poor child, she'll be heartbroken, I'm afraid. She and Basil were devoted to one another. Fancy that doctor turning everyone out of the house. He must have thought that there was something very wrong. Do you think it can have been the drains?"

Arnold made a feeble attempt to stem this flow of words. "Have you been to Forstal Farm recently, Miss Maplewood?" he asked.

"I? Oh, dear, no. I'm not very interested in cows and pigs and things like that. They're so terribly unintellectual. I often wonder what a clever man like Geoffrey sees in them. But a man must have some interest outside his business, mustn't he? Besides, my work as Lady Patroness of the I.I.I. keeps me so dreadfully busy. But I did go with Geoffrey to attend the Harvest Festival last year. The Vicar asked me to go particularly, and I didn't like to refuse, for I think he's so deserving although he is so terribly low church. But I didn't like the service and the church smelt too dreadfully of onions. I was really quite glad when it was all over."

"It must have been very trying," said Arnold sympathetically. "Did you see Mr. Basil Maplewood yesterday?"

"No. Geoffrey met him at the station and drove him straight to Tenteridge. We didn't know definitely that he was coming until he rang Geoffrey up on Friday morning. Of course, we'd asked him to come if he could possibly manage it, because he wanted to see something on the farm. Geoffrey can tell you what it was. He had a farm of his own at Hithering, you know. That's why he and Geoffrey always got on so well. They were both terribly interested in farming. It was quite different when poor Kenneth was alive. He used to let the farm to a dreadful man who did the most awful things. Never put any manure on the land, I've heard Geoffrey say. But, after all, perhaps one can't blame him for that. It does smell so terribly, don't you think?"

"It is certainly apt to be offensive," said Arnold politely. "Was Mr. Basil coming here before he went home?"

"Oh, yes, of course. He wouldn't have thought of being so close without coming to see his aunt. Saxby was to have fetched him and Geoffrey at three o'clock this afternoon. I simply couldn't understand it when Dukes rang up this morning to say that Geoffrey wanted the car at once. I felt sure there must be something the matter, for Geoffrey never comes home before Sunday afternoon, but Dukes rang off before I could question him about it. I didn't know what to do, for there was only roast mutton for lunch. Mutton always disagrees with Geoffrey. He suffers terribly from indigestion, poor dear. And, after all, he couldn't touch anything but a boiled egg and a little bread and butter."

At this moment the door opened and Geoffrey Maplewood entered the room. Fully dressed and shaved, he looked now more impressive than he had earlier that morning. Arnold saw before him a short, rather weedy-looking man of middle age wearing powerful glasses, with sharp features and a generally clever expression.

"Oh, there you are, dear," his sister exclaimed. "Feeling rested? That's right. And here's Inspector—oh, dear me, I'm afraid I've forgotten his name. My memory's awful. He wants to talk to you about poor dear Basil."

Arnold introduced himself afresh. "I shall be very grateful if you will tell me all you know of the tragic event at Tenteridge this morning, Mr. Maplewood," he continued.

Geoffrey Maplewood passed his hand wearily across his forehead. "I'll tell you all I can, readily enough," he replied. "But it all seems like some ghastly nightmare. I couldn't believe my own ears when the doctor told me that Basil was dead. It seemed impossible—quite impossible."

Arnold tactfully disregarded this. "I'd like to begin with yesterday, if you have no objection," he said. "You met your nephew at the station here, did you not?"

"Yes. He arrived by the two forty-five. I suggested to him some time ago that he should come to Forstal Farm and see a new disc harrow that I had recently bought.. On Friday morning I had a letter from him to say that he had been called up to London on business and asking if it would suit me for him to come here on Saturday for a couple of nights. I at once sent him a telegram saying that it would suit me perfectly."

"Your nephew knew that you were in the habit of spending the week-end at the farm?"

"It was because he knew that that he suggested coming here on Saturday afternoon. I met the train and we drove straight to the farm. We spent an hour or so watching the harrow and tractor at work and then walked to the house for tea. Neither Basil nor I left it again until. . . ." Mr. Maplewood's voice trailed away into silence.

"Of course you didn't go out again!" his sister exclaimed. "Whatever could you find to do in a place like Tenteridge? I always think the country's too terribly depressing especially at this time of year. Don't you, Inspector?"

"I'm rather fond of it myself," replied Arnold shortly. "Would you mind telling me how you spent the evening, Mr. Maplewood?"

"I don't know that we did anything in particular. Basil was very keen on farming, and he and I had a common interest. We discussed that subject for some time, and he also told me about the business which had called him to London, and asked my advice upon that matter. What with one thing and another, we had plenty to talk about."

"Did poor dear Basil tell you anything about Phoebe?" Miss Maplewood asked eagerly.

"We did not discuss her affairs," her brother replied shortly. "We had dinner in the ordinary way and then sat in the lounge till a little after ten, when we went to bed."

"Did you look round the house before you went upstairs, Mr. Maplewood?" Arnold asked.

"Why, of course he did!" Miss Maplewood exclaimed before her brother could speak. "You've no idea how fussy he is over things like that. You mightn't believe it, but even here he goes all round the house every night after the servants have gone to bed to see that everything's all right. Don't you, Geoffrey?"

Arnold sighed patiently. "Did you follow your usual custom last night, Mr. Maplewood?" he asked.

"I do not remember ever having failed to do so," Maplewood replied. "Before I went upstairs last night I went to the front door, locked and bolted it. Then I went to the back door to satisfy myself that Mrs. Dukes had locked it behind her. I then went to every room on the ground floor to see that the windows were properly secured. After that I went upstairs and looked at all the windows there. By that time Basil had gone to his room. I opened his door and asked him if he had everything he wanted. He told me he had, and we said good night. And that was the last time I spoke to him."

"Did you notice whether his bedroom window was open or shut?"

"He was in the act of opening it when I entered the room."

"And your own bedroom window, Mr. Maplewood?"

"I opened it myself before I went to bed."

"What about the windows in the bathroom, lavatory, landing and boxroom?"

"They were all shut and properly secured. I am perfectly sure of that."

"You say that you went into every room in the house, Mr. Maplewood. You are quite satisfied that there is no possibility of any unauthorised person having been concealed on the premises?"

"You don't think there can have been, do you, Inspector?" Miss Maplewood exclaimed excitedly. "One hears of such terrible things happening in lonely country places. Now that you've put the idea into my head, I shall always be terrified of a man getting into my bedroom at night."

Arnold glanced at her angular figure. "I don't think you need have any fears on that score, Miss Maplewood," he said feelingly.

"Of course not," replied her brother, answering Arnold's question. "Nobody could possibly have been hidden in the house yesterday evening."

"Could anyone have entered it during the night?"

"Only by climbing in through one of the two open windows. And I am perfectly sure that no one could have done this without waking me. I am an exceptionally light sleeper, and any unusual noise always awakens me."

"That's quite true, Inspector," Miss Maplewood interposed. "If a dog barks in the night, he's sure to hear it. Aren't you, Geoffrey?"

"Yes, my dear," replied her brother absently. "But last night I heard no unusual noise whatever. I woke soon after daylight, as I nearly always do, and soon after half-past seven I heard the baize door open, which told me that Mr. Dukes and her daughter had arrived."

"I don't altogether trust that girl," said Miss Maplewood darkly. "I'm quite sure I caught her making eyes at Saxby that time I was over there last year. And she must know well enough that Saxby is a married man with two children and a third coming in May."

"Mrs. Dukes brought you a cup of tea, did she not?" Arnold asked hastily.

"Yes, at eight o'clock punctually. I had forgotten to tell Basil overnight that he should have the first use of the bathroom, and I asked Mrs. Dukes to tell him this when she took him his tea. A minute or two later I heard their voices in his bedroom. Then at twenty minutes past eight—for I looked at my watch at the time—I heard Basil leave his room and walk whistling across the landing and go into the bathroom and slam the door behind him."

"Did you hear anything else, Mr. Maplewood?"

"I heard Basil turn on the bath water, and a few minutes later I heard him turn it off again. And, now that I think of it, I heard something that sounded like a car in the road with its engine running. And I certainly heard a heavy thud, but I couldn't tell where it came from. I suppose that Mrs. Dukes or her daughter must have dropped something. And it was just after that that I heard the car or whatever it was move off down the road."

"Can you tell me exactly when this was, Mr. Maplewood?"

"It must have been fully half-past eight by that time. I listened for Basil to come out of the bath room, but he seemed a very long time. I kept looking at my watch, rather impatiently, I'm afraid, for I had to have my own bath and get dressed and shaved by breakfast time. Breakfast was ordered for nine o'clock, and I always like to be strictly punctual. At last at ten minutes to nine I felt I couldn't wait any longer. I went to the bathroom door, knocked on it and called to Basil. But I couldn't get any answer, and so—"

"I know what happened after that, Mr. Maplewood," said Arnold, getting up from his chair. "I needn't trouble you any further just now."

"Oh, but you'll come and see us again, won't you, Inspector?" exclaimed Miss Maplewood volubly. "Before you leave Addleford I must take you round to the I.I.I. The inmates are just too sweet, and you'll love them. You will come if you can find time for it, won't you? It's such a deserving cause, and I'm quite sure you'll be interested. Are you really certain that you must go now? Well, good night, and don't forget your promise about the I.I.I."

Arnold disengaged himself at last. He drove to the police station, where he found the Superintendent waiting for him.

"Ah, here you are," said Garland. "You needn't worry about finding anywhere to sleep. My wife and I can put you up and feed you as long as you are in Addleford. Well, and how have you got on?"

"I'm very grateful for your offer," Arnold replied. "I don't fancy I shall impose upon your hospitality for very long, for up to the present I have no evidence whatever that a crime has been committed."

Garland nodded. "I warned you that it might turn cut to be a mare's nest," he remarked.

"I don't see any evidence of foul play so far. I've heard several accounts of what happened at the house this morning, and they all dovetail into one another with extraordinary accuracy. I've just come from Riverbank, where I hadn't the chance of saying much to Mr. Maplewood, for his sister wouldn't let us alone. I never heard a woman talk so much in my life. And what, by the way, is the I.I.I.?"

Garland slapped his knees and laughed uproariously. "The I.I.I.!" he exclaimed. "I'll bet you she asked you to visit the place. Didn't she?"

"The last thing she said to me was that I'd promised to," Arnold replied. "But I haven't."

"She'll get you there by hook or by crook, you'll see if she doesn't. And she won't be satisfied until you put at least a quid in the box. I.I.I. stands for the Institute of Incurable Imbeciles. It's Miss Maplewood's pet idea. She bought a house in the town, collected half a dozen half-witted country lassies whose parents were glad to get them off their hands, and put them into it. There's a matron and a consulting physician and all that, and Miss Maplewood calls herself the Lady Patroness. She duns everybody she meets for a subscription or a donation, and she won't let them go until she's got it."

"It's all quite square and above board, I suppose?"

"Oh, perfectly. But whether the Institute fulfils any really useful purpose, I very much doubt. What impression did Geoffrey Maplewood make upon you?"

"Not very much one way or the other," Arnold replied. "He answered my questions readily enough. What can you tell me about these people?"

"They're perfectly respectable and law-abiding, and I know nothing whatever against their reputation. They aren't natives of this town, you understand. It's like this: The Addle Paper Mill is a very old-established concern. It used to belong to some people called Seagood and Waverley. I don't know anything about the Waverleys, but the last Seagood died about a dozen years ago, and his family decided to sell the mill as a going concern.

"It was bought by two strangers, Mrs. Maplewood and Mr. Pelling. You've seen Maplewood for yourself. Pelling was a different sort of man entirely. He was several years younger than Maplewood, very fair, with an un-English but not bad-looking sort of face. People used to say that he had foreign blood in him somewhere.

"However that may be, he was a very clever paper maker and took charge of the technical side of the business. The mill wasn't doing wonderfully well when he and Maplewood bought it. But after awhile they began to produce a special sort of paper which is very largely used in the electrical industry, they tell me. Hermatine, they call it. And ever since that time the business has been prosperous enough."

"Pelling's name cropped up this afternoon while I was talking to the Dukes," Arnold remarked. "It seems that at one time he used to be pretty frequently with Maplewood at the house. Dukes wouldn't talk about him. He said I'd better ask Maplewood."

Garland nodded. "I dare say. Countrymen are usually pretty careful of what they say. Did you ask Maplewood about Pelling?"

"In view of Dukes' reticence, I didn't care to with his sister in the room."

"Just as well, perhaps. Well, I can give you Pelling's story in a few words. He and Maplewood were partners in the business. The firm's bank was the local branch of the South-Eastern Bank. All cheques over a certain amount had to be signed by both partners, though actually Maplewood was responsible for the financial side.

"One fine day one of the firm's cheques was presented to the bank. It was for the sum of £5,000, was drawn in favour of Pelling, and bore the signature of both partners. As it happened, payment of this cheque would have slightly overdrawn the firm's account. The bank manager, a personal friend of Maplewood's, sent him a note, and he went posthaste to the bank. On being shown the cheque, he stated that he had never set eyes on it before. I didn't tell you that the cheque was made out in Pelling's handwriting.

"Maplewood was utterly flabbergasted. He told the manager that he had always been on the best of terms with Pelling and simply couldn't understand the affair. He asked to be allowed to tear up the cheque and say no more about it. But that couldn't be done, for Pelling had passed the cheque through his private account at another bank, and some explanation would have to be made. The long and short of it was that the experts were called in, and for once they agreed. Underneath what looked very like Maplewood's signature there were definite traces of carbon from a carbon paper. Pelling had obviously traced Maplewood's signature on the cheque and then written with a pen over the tracing.

"That of course is where we came in. Pelling was arrested on a charge of forgery. A search was made and in his desk at the office were found some sheets of carbon paper with tracings of Maplewood's signature on them, a passport recently taken out and a first-class single ticket, available three days after the cheque was presented, from London to Amsterdam. It was one of the clearest cases one could hope for. Pelling was remanded for trial at the Assizes, where he got three years."

"Did his counsel put up any sort of defence?" Arnold asked.

"Yes, but neither the judge nor the jury took it very seriously. Pelling maintained that the £5,000 was due to him from the firm as a reward for his invention of Hermatine, but could produce no sort of agreement to that effect. His story was that Maplewood had given him a blank cheque already bearing his signature and asked him to fill it in, as he had injured his hand at the farm during the previous week-end. Evidence of such injury was available. Pelling also said that he had secured the passport, following Maplewood's suggestion that he should visit a number of Dutch paper mills. He was unable to find the witness who could confirm this. Finally he denied all knowledge of the ticket to Amsterdam and the carbon paper."

"Pretty thin, surely," Arnold remarked.

"Too thin to be of any use to him. The judge in his summing-up called it a very despicable attempt to defraud the partner who trusted him. Maplewood played up very well, I am bound to say. He raised enough money to repay Pelling what he had put into the business, and the partnership was dissolved. What became of Pelling, I don't know. All this happened five years ago, so he must have been out of jail for some time."

"The partnership was dissolved, you say," Arnold remarked. "Maplewood is now the sole owner of the mill, then. Has he any other interests, do you know?"

"Only the farm, so far as I am aware. He's a retiring sort of chap, and doesn't throw his weight about the town at all. Leaves that sort of thing to his sister. She's always in the limelight if there's anything going on locally."

"Are they pretty well liked?"

"Oh, yes, I think so. Maplewood has a reputation for driving pretty hard bargains, and some people think that his sister is a bit of a nuisance at times. But I dare say you know how it is in a little town like this. Nobody's ever perfect. While you were out this afternoon I put a call through to Staplemouth and had a chat with the super there. He gave me some facts about Maplewood's nephew. Care to hear them?"

"Rather," Arnold replied. "He plays a very important part in the affair after all."

Garland drew towards him a pad on which he had jotted down some notes. "Here you are, then," he said. "Basil Maplewood lived at Hithering Court, about five miles from Staplemouth. Very nice house, not too unwieldy, standing in a small park with a home farm attached. The Maplewood family have lived there for generations, and the property has always descended in the male line.

"We needn't go any further back than Bertram Maplewood, who had three children: Kenneth, the eldest, Geoffrey and Monica. Bertram died shortly after the war and was succeeded by his eldest son, Kenneth. Kenneth had two children, Basil and Phoebe. He died two years ago when Basil was twenty. Geoffrey acted as Basil's guardian until he came of age last year, when Basil inherited the property.

"Now, in addition to Hithering Court, the family owned two or three farms on the outskirts of Staplemouth. In recent years these farms have been developed as building land, very much to the family's advantage. From one source and another, the super at Staplemouth informed me that Basil's income can't have been less than £10,000 a year."

"Very nice, too," Arnold remarked.

"More than you or I shall ever earn, anyhow,"

Garland replied. "Basil seemed to have been a quiet, capable sort of young chap, fond of hunting and shooting and that sort of thing, and spending most of his time looking round the estate. I gather that his father had been rather inclined to let things go their own way, and that since he's been in the saddle Basil has tightened things up all round. Both he and his sister, Phoebe, are well liked locally."

"Miss Maplewood mentioned Phoebe when I was up at Riverbank just now," said Arnold thoughtfully. "Basil wasn't married, by any chance, was he?"

Garland shook his head. "No, nor even engaged, so far as my information goes," he replied.

"Then one would imagine that his sister inherits the estate?"

"One doesn't imagine anything of the kind," Garland replied with a significant smile. "Didn't I tell you that the property descended in the male line?"

It took a couple of seconds for the significance of this to dawn upon the Inspector.

"By Jove!" he exclaimed abruptly. "Then Geoffrey Maplewood is his nephew's heir?"

## CHAPTER FIVE

EARLY NEXT MORNING Lambert drove Arnold to Tenteridge. The Inspector's first call was upon Terry, who was just about to go on duty at the master's house.

Terry's inquiries had not been fruitless. "I know pretty well who's likely to be about on Sunday mornings, sir," he said. "But just to make sure, I had a chat with Mr. Vincent, who keeps the Maypole, and between us we made a list of the likely ones. I've spoken to them all, and two of them saw the van you spoke about, sir."

"Good work!" Arnold exclaimed. "Let's hear what they told you."

Terry produced his notebook. "The first of them is a young chap called Archie Pender, who works at Lees Farm. That's the next farm to Mr. Maplewood's, sir, on the other side of the village. Every Sunday morning Pender drives one of those three-wheeled motor milk-floats from Lees Farm to Tenteridge and back. He brings thirty gallons of milk or thereabouts to a man in the village who has a milk round.

"He has to be in the village about half-past eight sharp, for that's the time the man he delivers the milk to starts on his round. Yesterday he started from Lees Farm as usual and as he was getting towards the house he saw a tradesman's van pulled up outside, as he thought. But when he got up to it he saw that it wasn't standing at either of the gates, but somewhere between them. And he saw that the driver had got out and was doing something to the engine. Pender pulled up and asked him if he was all right, and the driver said that he'd only got some water in his carburetor and would have it drained in a couple of shakes, so Pender drove off. He hadn't thought any more about it until I spoke to him this morning."

"He couldn't tell you exactly what time it was that he saw the van, I suppose?" Arnold asked.

"Not exactly sir. But he knows he got to Tenteridge a minute or two before nine, for the man he delivers the milk to remarked upon it. It would take him two or three minutes from the house to

the village. He must have passed the house about five-and-twenty
minutes past eight, as near as I can judge. He was in the village a
matter of five or ten minutes picking up the empty churns from the
day before. And when he passed the house on his way back to
Lees Farm the van wasn't there."

"Did he give you any sort of description of the van or its
driver?"

"Nothing very definite, sir. He says that it was an old Morris,
sort of gray in colour and badly needed a coat of paint. There was-
n't any name on it that he could see. And all he remembers about
the number is that it only had two letters which shows that the van
wasn't exactly new. He didn't see the driver's face, but he's pretty
sure that he was wearing a dark coat and a leather cap and he
spoke like a Londoner."

"Do you know anyone in the neighbourhood who owns a van
of that description?"

"Well, sir, there are plenty of old Morris vans about, and some
of them look none too smart. But I couldn't say which of them this
was, sir."

"You couldn't be expected to," said Arnold. "Did Pender tell
you how the van was standing?"

"Yes, sir. Pulled well in to the left-hand side of the road looking towards the village. That's the side of the road the house
stands on. The van was close up against the garden wall."

"Was there anybody in it besides the driver?"

"Pender didn't see anybody, sir."

"Very well. Someone else saw the van as well, I understand."

"Yes, sir, another young chap of the name of Will Owens. His
father keeps the baker's shop in the village. He's got a girl who
lives about five miles away, and latterly he spends every Sunday
with her people. Yesterday he started up from the village on his
push-bike, a couple of minutes or so before half-past eight. He
says he's sure of the time, because he looked at his watch particularly. And I think he must be just about right, sir, because he says
that a few moments after he started out he saw Archie Pender pull
up with his milk-float.

"Owens cycled along the road towards Forstal Farm. He says
that he wasn't in any great hurry, for he didn't want to reach the
place where his girl lives before nine, so it took him a minute or
two over the half-hour to cover the five miles. When he came in
sight of the house he saw a van standing outside. The driver was
sitting in his seat doing something with a piece of rope, Owens

says. Just before he got to the van it started off and passed him going towards Tenteridge. Coming from the village, Owens wouldn't have seen the van until he was within a hundred yards or so of it, because of the curve in the road."

"What do you suppose the driver was doing with a piece of rope?" Arnold asked.

"I couldn't say, sir. Perhaps he'd used it for tying up something and was coiling it down again. I asked Owens if he had looked at the man, and he told me that he hadn't taken much notice of him. He saw that he was nobody he knew, and he thinks he was wearing a leather cap with flaps over the ears. And he's pretty sure he had a black moustache, but he says he's very doubtful if he'd recognize him again if he saw him."

"Did Owens take any notice of the van?"

"Not much, I'm afraid, sir. He couldn't tell me anything about the make or the number. But he said that it was a shabby old concern with a crack right across the windscreen."

"What do you estimate the time at which Owens saw it?"

"Well, sir, I reckon that at the pace he was going, that it would have taken him seven minutes or so to the house. It must have been as near as makes no matter, five-and-twenty minutes to nine when the van passed him."

"And you haven't found anybody else who saw this van?"

"Nobody else, sir. You see, most folks like to lie in bed a bit late on Sunday mornings. And if anybody in the village did happen to see a van drive through, they wouldn't be likely to take any particular notice. There's quite a lot of traffic comes through at one time and another."

"So I gather. By the way, there's a bus service along that road, isn't there? A bus passed me as I was walking to Forstal Farm yesterday afternoon."

"Yes, sir. But the first bus on Sundays doesn't leave Tenteridge until a quarter-past ten."

"That's no good, then. You know Dukes pretty well, I suppose, Terry? What's your opinion of him?"

"I don't think anyone could ever say a word against Dukes or any of his family, sir. He's lived in these parts all his life, and was bailiff of Forstal Farm before Mr. Maplewood bought the place. Mrs. Dukes was in service at the Vicarage when he married her, and I've always heard her very highly spoken of."

Arnold gave Terry a lift to the house and then proceeded to make certain investigations on his own account. Two witnesses at

least—Pender and Hetty Dukes—were agreed as to the position of
the van. Standing close to the garden wall and roughly half-way
between the two gates, Arnold discovered that from this spot, owing to the height and thickness of the shrubbery, nothing could be
seen of the house but the roof. On the opposite side of the road
was a low bank. Standing on this he could see, above the top of the
shrubbery, two of the upper windows of the house, those of the
boxroom and bathroom.

His next experiment entailed the assistance of Terry. He instructed the constable to enter the bathroom, open the window as
wide as possible and walk about the floor. Arnold then took up the
most favourable point of observation on the low bank. Even from
here, owing to the height of the window above the floor, he could
see very little of the interior of the room. Terry only became visible when he came close up to the window and actually looked out.

Arnold's next concern was to examine the space between the
garden wall and the side of the house. The shrubbery came close
up to the former, in fact, the upper branches overhung it and had
recently been trimmed back. Between the shrubbery and the wall
of the house was a narrow space, two feet wide. The window of
the bathroom was vertically above that of the dining-room. On
either side of these windows pipes ran to the ground. On the right
was the soil pipe from the lavatory. On the left were the waste
pipes from the bath and the washbasin. These were of lead, and
terminated a short distance above the ground level. They discharged into a cemented gully. Arnold decided that although it
might be possible for an exceptionally agile person to climb up to
the bathroom window by the aid of the pipe, there was no sign of
the feat having been attempted. He measured the distance from the
top of the bathroom window to the top of the garden wall and
found it to be thirty-eight feet.

The ground between the shrubbery and the wall of the house
was hard and dry. But on going round to the western side of the
house Arnold found that a wide flower-bed ran along the whole of
its length. The soil in this bed was soft and moist and would have
shown the slightest sign of disturbance. Anyone attempting to
climb up to the windows of either of the bedrooms must necessarily have left traces on the flower-bed.

Continuing his examination of the outside of the house, Arnold
noticed one method by which it could be entered with comparative
ease. The porch was a substantial affair, supported on its outer side
on two brick pillars. Immediately above the porch was the landing

window. It would not be a very difficult matter to clamber up one of the pillars and so reach the roof of the porch, which was covered with lead. If the landing window happened to be open, it would merely be a matter of getting through it into the house. But, according to all the available evidence, the landing window had been shut and fastened during the whole of the night preceding the tragedy.

Having satisfied his curiosity as to these points, Arnold went into the house and began to make a minute examination of each room. Bearing in mind Dr. Prescott's remark about the complete absence of any electrical apparatus, he made a special search for these. He found the calor gas cylinder installed in the scullery, with connections to the gas stove and to burners in every room in the house. But of any form of electrical device there was no trace. Not even a pocket torch or a gas lighter. The front doorbell was of the clockwork type which rings alarmingly on the inner side of the panel when the button is pressed.

Arnold went into the bathroom, which had not been touched since his previous visit, sat down on the edge of the bath and lighted his pipe. He had to decide whether the shabby Morris van and its driver had any connection with the death of Basil Maplewood.

To begin with, there seemed very little doubt that the thud heard by the occupants of the house had been the sound of Basil's body falling to the ground. It was generally agreed that the noise had been heard within a couple of minutes either way of half-past eight. The evidence seemed to show that the van had been standing outside the house at five-and-twenty minutes past eight and had driven away ten minutes later. It had then been a short distance from the bathroom window to the time of Basil's death.

But any theory involving the responsibility of the driver for this death raised a number of insuperable difficulties. Basil had undoubtedly died when he was in the act of getting into his bath. While in that position he was absolutely invisible from any point in the road—or, for that matter, in the grounds of the house. Every statement which had been made pointed to the extreme improbability of anyone having entered the house unseen. Even if the house had been entered, the door of the bathroom was locked inside, and there were no other means of access.

Actually there was nothing definitely suspicious about the van or its driver, beyond the fact that it was standing outside the house at the time of Basil's death. A van, especially an old crock, is always liable to minor breakdowns. As Terry had pointed out, vehicles of all classes used this particular road in respectable numbers. The driver might indeed have got some water into his carburetor and pulled up outside the house to drain it out. And it must be remembered that of the three witnesses, two—Hetty Dukes and Archie Pender—had seen him bending over the engine, and one, Will Owens, had seen him in the driving seat. There was no suggestion that he had ever left the van at all.

Resolving the matter in his mind, Arnold came to the conclusion that the crime, if crime had been committed, must have originated nearer home. For the present the question of the motive must be left out of the reckoning. But was it not significant that Basil's death had occurred while he was his uncle's guest?

It was ridiculous to imagine the guilt of any member of the Dukes' family. Basil had been scarcely known to them, and had certainly played no part in any of their lives. Eliminating the Dukes, it might be said that Basil had been alone with his uncle for several hours before his death. And if some subtle death-trap had been laid for him, his uncle had had ample opportunity to prepare it during the night. Neither Mrs. Dukes nor Hetty had entered the bathroom on Sunday morning. And Geoffrey Maplewood had sent a message to his nephew by Mrs. Dukes that he should use the bathroom first.

The Inspector relighted his pipe, which had gone out, and puffed at it vigorously for a few seconds. The germ of an idea was struggling for expression. What sort of a death-trap could Geoffrey Maplewood have set during the night? For the twentieth time at least Arnold cast his eyes round the bathroom, until they fell upon the gas bracket fixed to the wall beside the basin. And then with a gleam of sudden inspiration he asked himself if therein lay the answer to the riddle. Had Geoffrey Maplewood turned on the tap and filled the room with gas? Had his nephew been overcome by the poisonous atmosphere thus created?

For the moment Arnold believed that he had solved the problem, until the many objections to his theory poured in a confused stream into his mind. He tried to discipline these into some sort of order.

The least sensitive nose would have detected the presence of the gas. Yet Basil had entered the bathroom and locked the door behind him. Reuben had noticed no offensive smell when he had forced the door open.

Basil had remained at least ten minutes in the room before he was overcome. During this period he had shaved, an operation he could not have performed if he had been inhaling gas all the time.

Dr. Prescott would surely have recognized the symptoms of gas-poisoning when he examined the body.

In disgust Arnold got up and, after a final survey of the bathroom, proceeded to search the rest of the house for some vestige of a clue. He was thus engaged when a farm cart drew up outside and Reuben appeared with the top of a trestle table, which he carried up to the landing. He greeted the Inspector as an old friend. "Still at work, then, I see," he said.

"Yes, still at work," Arnold replied. "Look here, Dukes, do you know anything about this calor gas installation?"

"Oh, yes, for I've always looked after it since Mr. Maplewood had it put in a couple of years back," Reuben replied. "Not that there's anything much to look after, for that matter. The gas comes in cylinders, and as soon as one's getting empty, I ring up the calor people. They bring a full one along, disconnect the empty one and put the full one in its place. It's a very good idea where there's no gas or electricity laid on. Mr. Maplewood has always found it most satisfactory. It saves a lot of work with lamps and it's better than ordinary gas, they say, because it isn't poisonous."

Arnold saw the last substance of his precious theory vanish into thin air.

"Oh, it isn't poisonous, is it?" he said. "By the way, you've got an electric plant at the farm, haven't you?"

"Yes, and very handy it is. Mr. Maplewood put it in when he first bought the place. It's a paraffin engine driving a dynamo direct with a storage battery. One of the chaps looks after it and it never gives any trouble."

"I wonder Mr. Maplewood never thought of bringing the current along here."

"He did think of it at one time, but when he found out what it would cost to carry the wires from the farm to here, he didn't do any more about it. He said he'd wait until the electric light company brought their cable along this road from the village. When that'll be, I can't say. But it isn't as if Mr. Maplewood lived here all the time. He's only here for one night in the week."

A car drew up outside and Arnold left the house to meet it. It was driven by Superintendent Garland and contained as passengers Dr. Prescott and a tall elderly man whom Arnold recognized as Dr. Hallam, a pathologist employed by the Home Office. After mutual greetings, the four entered the house, Dr. Hallam carrying a bulky attaché case.

"We'll go straight up to the room where the body is," said Dr. Prescott briskly. "Do you happen to know if Dukes has brought that table along, Inspector?"

"Yes, you'll find it on the landing. Do you want any help with it?"

"No, thanks. Dr. Hallam and I can manage very well between us."

The two medical men went upstairs, leaving Arnold and the Superintendent standing in the hall.

"I don't think I should relish the job of cutting up dead bodies," said the latter. "Look here, I can't wait while they're carving slices off the joint. I've got to get back to Addleford to attend a special meeting of the Bench. You won't mind if Lambert drives the pathologist back in your car?"

"Not a bit. I shall probably come back with him when I've heard what the doctors have to say."

"Just as well. There's a lady wants to see you most particularly. I told her I'd ring her up when you got back to Addleford."

"A lady!" Arnold exclaimed. "Don't for mercy's sake tell me it's Miss Maplewood!"

"Not Miss Monica Maplewood, though I dare say she'll be on your track before long. This one's her niece, Miss Phoebe Maplewood. She's come all the way from Staplemouth with rather a queer yarn. Better hear it for yourself. Well, so-long."

The Superintendent hurried away, leaving Arnold to his own devices. Reuben had gone back to the farm in his cart and the Inspector was alone in the house, but for the doctors at their task behind the closed doors of the bedroom upstairs. Arnold opened the baize door and passed through into the back premises.

The thin smoke of his theory was still drifting through his brain. He walked into the scullery and stared at the calor gas cylinder. As Reuben had said, the whole affair was simple enough. The cylinder stood in a corner connected by a screwed union to a system of fine pipes which radiated to the different parts of the house. Arnold saw that it would be the easiest thing in the world to unscrew the union, remove the cylinder and replace it by another. But if the confounded stuff wasn't poisonous—?

And then all at once his theory returned in full force, but with a vital alteration. It was so conspicuously simple to remove one cylinder and replace it by another. And what if the second cylinder contained, not the innocuous calor gas, but something else?

Arnold's knowledge of toxicology was by no means profound. He was aware that lethal gases existed, though he was ignorant of their exact properties. He could imagine an odourless gas of which the first effects would be inappreciable, but which would prove fatal if inhaled long enough. In the light of this inspiration he proceeded to reconstruct his theory.

On some previous occasion, Geoffrey Maplewood had brought to the house a cylinder of poison gas which he had hidden in some convenient place. If the gas were sufficiently lethal only a small cylinder would be required. Late on Saturday night or early on Sunday morning he had got out of bed by the light, not of the gas, but of an electric torch. Where was the torch? He had taken it back to Addleford in his pocket, of course.

On getting out of bed, he had taken the container from its hiding-place and carried it to the scullery. There he had disconnected the calor gas cylinder and replaced it by the poison container. He had then gone upstairs to the bathroom and turned on the tap of the gas bracket. He had left this tap on until he judged the container to be empty. Then he returned to the scullery and put the calor gas cylinder back in its place. Having once more hidden the container, he had returned to bed.

Arnold was so pleased with this theory that he spent an hour or more searching unsuccessfully for the container of his imagination. At the end of this period he heard voices on the landing, and a few moments later the two doctors came downstairs.

Dr. Prescott explained that he must hurry off to attend to his patients, and Arnold was left alone with Dr. Hallam. He and the pathologist had met frequently on previous occasions. He had therefore no hesitation in putting the question to him at once. "Well, Doctor, what was the cause of that poor fellow's death?"

The pathologist looked at him over his glasses. "You policemen are incorrigible," he replied irritably. "You seem to think that pathology is an exact science like mathematics. You expect an investigation into the cause of death to be like a sum which adds up to only one possible answer. But let me tell you, my friend, it isn't as easy as that. Death doesn't always leave his signature behind to be read infallible like your people profess to be able to read finger marks."

"Sorry, Doctor," said Arnold apologetically. "I didn't mean to be tactless. I should have asked you for your opinion, of course."

The pathologist's features relaxed. "Oh, that's all right," he replied. "Only one does get tired sometimes of you people expecting a definite expression of facts. The best we can do is to examine the material before us and give an honest opinion based upon what we find. My opinion, for what it is worth, is that Basil Maplewood died as the result of shock."

"Shock!" repeated Arnold incredulously. "What sort of shock, Doctor?"

The pathologist shrugged his shoulders. "That surely is a matter for you to discover rather than me," he replied. "If you read any of the text-books on forensic medicine you will meet with many incidences of shock causing death without producing any post-mortem appearances. And I can assure you that our examination of the body upstairs has disclosed no reason for sudden death.

"In cases of this kind, especially where death has occurred in a bathroom, one looks first for some electrical contact as the most likely cause of death. People have been killed by touching defective electrical apparatus with their wet hands. But in this case Dr. Prescott assures me that the house contains no source of electricity whatever."

"That's quite true," said Arnold. "I've searched the whole place through and through and I can't find so much as a bell-push."

"Severe mental shock has been known to cause death, as have blows apparently so slight as to leave no post-mortem traces."

"Do you agree with Dr. Prescott that the bruises found on the body could not have caused death?"

The pathologist smiled. "After my long experience as an expert witness on such cases, I should hesitate to commit myself to that extent," he replied. "I prefer to confine myself to explaining the probabilities, rather than to make a definite assertion. The bruises you mention show that Basil Maplewood fell on the bathroom floor. It is possible that this fall was due to his bare feet slipping on the rubber floor covering. The injuries caused by this fall are not of themselves sufficient to have resulted in death. It is, I suppose, remotely possible that the shock of the fall could have caused death. But our examination has shown Basil Maplewood to have been exceptionally healthy. I leave it to you to judge of the likelihood of an ordinary fall causing the death of a young man in the enjoyment of perfect health."

"It doesn't sound very likely," Arnold agreed. "You're perfectly satisfied, however, that death was due to shock?"

"My dear man, I'm rarely, if ever, perfectly satisfied. There's no such thing as absolute finality in my profession. I can only tell you that the elimination of every other cause of death leaves shock as the only reasonable alternative."

"There's no possibility of his having been poisoned, I suppose?" Arnold suggested diffidently.

"At present a very remote possibility exists," the pathologist replied. "Practically every poison known to science leaves traces which can be observed by the expert on post-mortem examination. In this case, no such traces exist. But, as a matter of routine, I have removed portions of certain organs which I shall subject to analyses. May I ask what makes you suggest poison?"

"Oh, I don't know; the closed room and the gas bracket in it, perhaps."

The pathologist shook his head. "You can put gas poisoning out of your mind. It's always unmistakable. There was a teacup with a few dregs of tea in it by the bedside. I've taken what liquid there was left, and I propose to analyze it. I've even taken a sample of water from the bath. I'll let you know the result of my analyses in a few days from now."

And with that Arnold had to be content.

## CHAPTER SIX

**A**RNOLD RETURNED in the car to Addleford, and after dropping Dr. Hallam at the railway station, lunched frugally at a local grill-room. His hunger satisfied, he sought the company of Superintendent Garland, to whom he repeated his conversation with the pathologist.

"I've known Hallam for many years now," he said. "And I've found that it's almost impossible to pin him down to a definite statement. These experts are all alike. But it's his opinion that Basil Maplewood died of shock."

"What does he mean by that?" Garland demanded. "What sort of shock?"

"That's just what I asked him, and he had the nerve to say that it was up to me to find out. He said that the shock might have been mental or physical. What sort of a shock does a man get when he steps into his bath?"

"A most unpleasant one if the water's cold," Garland replied. "I know that, for my governor always made me have a cold bath every morning when I was a kid. But this particular bath wasn't so cold, was it?"

"Dr. Prescott said that the water was still warm when he felt it. But I'm pretty sure of one thing. If a shock was responsible for the fellow's death, it must have been an accidental one. I mean that no one else could possibly have administered it."

"You say you're perfectly sure of that?"

"Absolutely certain. I've been over that blessed house inside and out until I know it by heart. There are only two openings to the bathroom: the doorway with a heavy old-fashioned door, and a window only one pane of which is made to open.

"Now we know that at the time of Basil's death the door was locked on the inside. We can't be quite so sure about the window; later it was found slightly open, the first hole of the rod being on the peg. Geoffrey Maplewood says that he knows that it was shut and fastened on the previous evening. My own idea is that Basil opened it when he went into the bathroom on Sunday morning.

"As a matter of fact, the state of the window isn't of great importance, and that for two reasons. I'm quite satisfied that nobody could have seen Basil through it, even if it had been wide open, from any point outside. And the opening, even if the window was thrown back to the fullest possible extent, is so small that only a child could get through it.

"Now you see how it is! It's quite impossible that anyone should have got into the bathroom after Basil had locked himself in. There is no place in the bathroom where anyone could have hidden before then. Even supposing the miraculous presence of some intruder, how could he have brought off a sudden shock? Basil was a hefty young chap. He would have resisted and there would have been signs of a struggle. And how did his assailant escape? Not by the window, I'll wager my pension on that. And not by the door, obviously."

"Accidental death, do you think, then?"

"It looks precious like it. There's just one possibility which occurred to me while I was at the house this morning, but we'll have to wait till we hear further from Hallam before we talk about that. In the meantime, it might be well to consider how many people knew in advance that Basil would be at the house on Sunday morning."

"His uncle and aunt knew, of course," Garland remarked.

"Yes, they knew all right. Geoffrey Maplewood's statement is to the effect that Basil sent him a letter about coming down, which he received on Friday morning. Before that a visit had been suggested, but no date had been fixed. Geoffrey in turn rang up Dukes and passed on the information to him. It was probably generally known in the village by Friday afternoon. How many people Basil himself told about what he meant to do, we can't say."

"He said nothing about it to his sister, or so she declares," Garland replied. "By the way, I think I'd better ring her up and tell her that you're here."

"She's staying at Riverbank, I suppose?"

"No, she isn't. No doubt she'll tell you why for herself. She's at the Royal Hotel not more than a few hundred yards from here. I'll put a call through to her now."

As a result of a short conversation on the telephone, Garland was able to tell Arnold that Miss Phoebe Maplewood would come along straight away.

"She seems a sensible sort of girl," he added. "And she's got her wits about her, too. And if you believe all she tells you, you may find cause to change the opinion you expressed just now."

"She's got her own theory to account for her brother's death, I suppose?"

"I wouldn't say that exactly. But she's got some startling suggestions to make about motive. However, I don't want to prejudice you. You'll form your own conclusions from what she says."

The announcement that Miss Phoebe Maplewood had arrived at the police station put an end to this conversation. Garland gave orders that she was to be admitted, and she appeared. Having said a few formal words of greeting and introduced her to Arnold, Garland murmured some excuse and left the room.

Arnold found himself confronted by a girl of twenty whose face bore a striking likeness to that of the dead man. She had a frank, open expression and a deep melodious voice. Arnold felt instinctively that though her judgment might be hasty and her prejudices unfounded, both would be based on straightforward honesty.

She had flung herself carelessly into a chair, and gazed at the Inspector with questioning gray eyes.

"I suppose you've heard what I told Mr. Garland this morning," she said simply.

"No, Miss Maplewood, I haven't," Arnold replied. "I wanted you to tell me about it for yourself. But you won't mind if I ask you a few questions first, will you? To begin with, how did you hear of your brother's death?"

"Aunt Monica rang me up on Sunday morning. I live at Hithering Court, you know. But when the message came I'd gone out to lunch. I hadn't told any of the servants where I should be, so of course they couldn't find me. As it happened, I didn't come home till seven o'clock, and I was told about what had happened. So I jumped into the car and drove straight here."

"You went to see your uncle and aunt, no doubt?"

Her eyes flashed angrily. "I did," she replied. "Uncle Geoff had gone to bed. He always manages to keep out of the way when there's any trouble. But I got the whole story out of Aunt Monica, and I told her pretty straight what I thought about it. I don't care if Geoffrey Maplewood is my uncle. Basil was my brother, and I'm the only one left to avenge him."

Though her words might be theatrical, her manner was no more than reasonably impulsive. She was obviously labouring under some deep emotion which she found difficult to express in appropriate words.

"Of course I wasn't going to stop at Riverbank," she continued. "I left Aunt Monica to think over what I'd said and went and took a room at the Royal. And then this morning I come and told Mr. Garland all about it. I wanted to go over to Tenteridge, but he said I'd better not. He told me the doctors were there and—"

She brushed her hand rapidly across her face. "It's too utterly beastly!" she exclaimed. "I just can't bear to think of Basil being dead and all the horrible things they are doing to him. They've found out by now how he was killed, of course?"

Arnold shook his head. "I'm afraid they haven't, Miss Maplewood," he replied swiftly.

"They haven't found out?" she exclaimed in angry incredulity. "But I thought that was what postmortems were for."

"They don't always result in determining the cause of death. For the present, your brother's accident remains a complete mystery."

She stared at Arnold, as though doubting whether she had heard him properly. "Accident!" she exclaimed. "It was a cowardly murder; you know that well enough."

"Can you prove it, Miss Maplewood?" Arnold asked gently.

"Of course I can prove it," she replied scornfully. "Basil was staying with Geoffrey alone when it happened, wasn't he?"

"That's no proof, I'm afraid. When your brother died he was alone in a locked bathroom which no one else could have entered."

"Oh, that's nonsense. Geoffrey must have got in somehow and killed him when he wasn't looking."

Evidently Phoebe Maplewood's mind was made up and would brook no argument. Arnold resolved to try a different tack. "Why should you believe that your uncle is a criminal, Miss Maplewood?"

"The fact that Geoffrey happens to be my uncle has nothing to do with it," she replied sharply. "Don't you see that he had everything to gain by my brother's death? Now, I suppose he won't have to pay back the money he borrowed."

"What money, Miss Maplewood?"

"Why, the money he borrowed from my father and never paid back. You know all about that, of course?"

"I'd like to hear your version of the story, Miss Maplewood," Arnold replied tactfully.

"Oh, I know all about it, because Basil told me. He always used to talk to me about the family business. It was long ago when Mr. Pelling bought the paper mill and came to live here. Geoffrey hadn't got any money of his own, or very little, and he had to borrow some to pay for his share of the business. Ten thousand pounds it was, Basil told me."

Arnold nodded. "And this sum has never been repaid?" he remarked.

"Not a penny piece of it. He's paid interest on it, but only a measly three per cent. My father wouldn't ask him any more. He thought it was his duty to help his brother as much as he could, I suppose. And that wasn't all, for when his partner was sent to prison and Geoffrey wanted to buy him out of the business, he borrowed another seven thousand."

"Had your brother taken any steps to get this money repaid since your father's death?"

"Not until quite recently. And then when Basil wanted ten thousand pounds all at once, he didn't see why Geoffrey shouldn't let him have it."

"I hope you won't mind if I ask you what your brother wanted this money for?"

"He wanted it for me," Phoebe Maplewood replied quickly. "I'm going to be married this summer, you see."

"Allow me to congratulate you, Miss Maplewood. Your brother was going to give you ten thousand pounds as a wedding present, I take it?"

"That's it. That's what Basil went up to London for on Thursday. He was going to see old Mr. Rustwick, who'd been our family lawyer for years and knew all about it. He wanted his advice as to the best way of getting the money out of Geoffrey."

"Did your brother mean to come here after he had seen the lawyer?"

"He hadn't made up his mind. When he left Hithering Court, he told me that it depended upon what Mr. Rustwick said. He had an invitation from Geoffrey to see some new gadgets he'd got on his farm. And Basil told me that he could use that as an excuse to see Geoffrey and talk to him about the money if Mr. Rustwick advised him to. I didn't know that Basil had decided to come here until the midday post on Saturday. He posted me a line on Friday night and told me that he was going to stay at Forstal Farm over the weekend, and would be home on Monday. Today, that is."

"Your uncle now becomes the owner of the estate, I understand?"

"Of course he does!" she exclaimed impatiently. "Don't you see? He's kept all Basil's money, and he won't even have to give back the seventeen thousand he borrowed. And I shan't get the ten thousand that Basil promised me, you may be sure of that. Aunt Monica has never approved of my marriage, and she'll see I don't get anything."

"Does anyone but your uncle benefit by your brother's death, Miss Maplewood?"

She shook her head violently. "Not a soul," she replied. "How could they? And it's simply silly to think of anyone having a grudge against him. Everyone who knew Basil was very proud of him. He hadn't an enemy in the world. I'm sure of that. It's as clear as anything could be that that crook Geoffrey killed him. And I shall tell him so to his face when I see him."

"You must on no account do anything of the kind, Miss Maplewood," said Arnold severely. "What you tell me is, of course, in the strictest confidence. But you mustn't disclose your suspicions to anyone else. It would do no possible good and might get you into very serious trouble indeed. You won't stay on here in Addleford, I suppose?"

"Oh, yes, I shall," she replied firmly. "I shall stay on at the Royal. I've got enough money for that. I'm not going to leave here till I know that Basil is going to be avenged."

It seemed to Arnold that this very determined young woman would present grave problems if uncontrolled. "You promise not to see your uncle and aunt without telling me first?" he said persuasively.

"I don't see why I should promise you anything," she replied with more than a hint of defiance in her tone.

"Well, perhaps not. But after all, you know, I do represent the police. I might have you locked up for threatening to cause a disturbance of the peace."

She smiled faintly at this. "I don't think you'll do that, somehow," she replied. "All right, I'll promise. But I don't see why I shouldn't tell Geoffrey and Aunt Monica what I think of them."

"My dear young lady, when you reach my age you'll know that it's very rarely any use telling people what you think of them. It doesn't alter their opinions in the slightest. I'm very glad of your promise, though. Now, if you find yourself in any difficulty, or if you think of anything we ought to know, come and see Mr. Garland or me at once."

After a few more words in the course of which Arnold secured the address of Mr. Rustwick the lawyer, Phoebe Maplewood left the police station. Garland must have watched her go out, for a minute or two later he joined Arnold.

"Well, what do you make of the youngest of the Maplewoods?" he asked.

"I think she will manage to keep her prospective husband in his place," Arnold replied. "But in spite of her somewhat impulsive youth, I rather took to her. She's one of those people who don't mince matters, at all events."

"If her facts are correct, there's a motive ready made for you," Garland said.

"I shall take steps to check up the facts, of course. On the face of it, it looks as if Geoffrey Maplewood had a lot to gain by murdering his nephew. But it altogether beats me how he did it. Or how anyone else did it, for that matter."

As Garland was about to reply, the telephone bell interrupted him. He took the call and frowned.

"There's her aunt, Miss Monica Maplewood," he said. "She's in the waiting-room now, and wants to see me. What about it?"

"Oh, we shall have to see her, I suppose," Arnold replied with a sigh. "And there are people, I believe, who envy a policeman's life."

Garland gave the necessary instructions, and a few moments later Miss Monica's voice could be heard in a voluble monologue as she was escorted along the passage. The door opened and she appeared. She was silent for a moment as she gazed eagerly round the room. And then she broke out afresh.

"Oh, it's true, then, what that man at the desk told me. The poor dear girl isn't here. But of course you know where she is. I've spent all day trying to find out what has become of her. She was terribly overwrought last night, and I was so afraid that she might do something dreadful. But just now somebody told me that she was at the Royal, and when I asked there they told me that she had come round here. I must find her at once and take her home with me. I can't bear to think of her all alone amongst strangers, especially just now. Why, you know, she hardly knows a soul in the town."

Garland managed to get a word in. "If you mean Miss Phoebe Maplewood, she left here barely five minutes ago," he said.

"Then I must just have missed her. It's very provoking, because I really can't think what people will say. It looks so odd for her to be staying at the Royal when Geoffrey and I are only too anxious to make her happy and comfortable at home. Besides, that dreadful man might follow her here, and it would be too terrible if they stayed at the same hotel. I should never be able to look any of my friends in the face again."

"What dreadful man, Miss Maplewood?" Garland asked incautiously.

"Oh, of course, you wouldn't know. Geoffrey and I have never said anything about it, for we always hoped that something would happen to prevent it before it was too late. I'm sure that if poor dear Basil had talked to her properly, she would have seen how impossible it was. But he and Phoebe were only children, after all, and they couldn't be expected to understand these things as we do. Kenneth would never have allowed it, I'm quite sure of that. It was a terrible blow to us when he died so suddenly. I didn't think Geoffrey would ever get over it. He was absolutely devoted to his brother, you know."

"I understand that Miss Phoebe is engaged to be married this year," Garland observed as Miss Maplewood paused for breath.

"That's just what I'm telling you about. Only with a child of her age, there's always a hope that she'll think better of it. Why, all our ancestors would turn in their graves if she walked out of Hithering Church on that man's arm. It isn't so much that he hasn't got any money. It's his impertinence in thinking himself fit to marry into the family. Just fancy! I remember him as a dirty little boy going to board school. And he didn't always touch his cap if one spoke to him, either. Mind you, I haven't a word to say against his father, though he does talk the broadest Hampshire you ever heard. So terribly uncouth, you know."

"His father, Miss Maplewood?" suggested Arnold.

"Yes, his father, Arthur Bingham. William is his youngest son, I've heard Phoebe speak of him as Bill. So terribly vulgar don't you think? Arthur Bingham—Mr. Bingham, as we were always taught to call him—is a most respectable man. He has been manager of the Hithering Court Estate ever since I can remember. And he has never presumed on his position in the least. My father always used to have him to lunch on Saturdays, and he behaved beautifully. Of course, we were careful not to have any other visitors. They mightn't have liked to sit down to table with a person of that class, you see. But Mr. Bingham is a true Christian. He was taught his catechism and knew how to do his duty in that state of life which it had pleased God to call him. I can't understand how he ever allowed his son William to get such an idea into his head. Why, it would have been just as reasonable if poor dear Basil had wanted to marry Hetty Dukes. But now I really must go to the Royal Hotel and see Phoebe. I'm quite sure I shall be able to persuade her to be reasonable."

She rose impulsively from her chair, but Arnold reached the door before she did, barring her exit. "Excuse me, Miss Maplewood," he said. "But if I were you *I* shouldn't see your niece just now."

"Not see Phoebe!" Miss Maplewood exclaimed indignantly. "Why not, if you please? I'm her nearest relation now that poor dear Basil's dead, you must remember. And though she's never been in any way an affectionate child, she must be in need of an aunt's love and consolation in her bereavement."

"I don't believe that in her present mood Miss Phoebe is in need of anything of the kind," Arnold replied sternly. "No doubt when she has got over the first shock she will come to Riverbank on her own accord."

"Well, perhaps you're right," said Miss Maplewood grudgingly. "She certainly said such terrible things last night. Really shocking things, which I couldn't possibly repeat. So unlike what one would expect from a Maplewood. That's what comes of her associating with that dreadful Bingham boy, I suppose. Why, she even seems to think that poor Geoffrey, who wouldn't harm a soul, is in some way responsible for Basil's death."

"While she thinks that, wouldn't it be better to leave her to her own devices?" Arnold suggested.

Miss Maplewood shook her head forebodingly. "It all seems very wrong," she replied. "But if you really think it best, I won't try to see her today at least. Dear me, how time flies. I promised to be at the I.I.I. not later than four o'clock I must dash along there at once. Oh, that reminds me, Inspector. You told me you'd like to see over the place, didn't you? Do come along now. I've got Saxby waiting with the car outside."

"I should enjoy nothing better, Miss Maplewood," said Arnold as he opened the door for her. "But, unfortunately, I'm under the Superintendent's orders and he has told me that I must stay in this office for the rest of the day."

Miss Maplewood turned to Garland with a winning smile. "But surely you could spare him for half an hour or so. It wouldn't take longer than that, really it wouldn't."

The Superintendent shook his head. "Duty must always come before pleasure, Miss Maplewood," he replied. "I have a lot of pressing work for the Inspector to do, and I simply can't spare him for a moment."

"Well, it will have to be some other time, then." And with evident reluctance she floated from the room, to be escorted to the car by the waiting sergeant.

When she had gone, Arnold produced his pouch, and, as he filled his pipe, sighed with relief. "Thanks for backing me up so nobly," he said. "I couldn't think of any other excuse on the spur of the moment. That woman's a regular mine of information. But most of what she brings to the surface is dross, I'm afraid, with a very minute speck of the true metal here and there. I hope for everybody's sake she won't start nagging her niece for a bit."

"Do you suppose that she knows more about this business than she cared to tell us?" the Superintendent asked.

"I don't think so. I can't imagine her keeping anything a secret for more than five minutes or so. She'd have an irresistible impulse to blurt it out to the first person she met. I'll ask something in turn. Do you suppose that Miss Phoebe's private affairs have got any bearing on the business?"

"That's just what I've been wondering. But I don't altogether see how they could. If we take her statements at their face value, her brother had no objection to her marriage, though her aunt and possibly her uncle are bitterly opposed to it. But Miss Phoebe strikes me as the sort of young woman who would be encouraged than otherwise by opposition."

"There's that little matter of the ten thousand she was expecting," Arnold remarked significantly.

"Yes, she won't get it now, I'm afraid. I wonder if it's a fact that Geoffrey Maplewood owes the estate seventeen thousand?"

"I'm very much inclined to go and see that lawyer chap. I dare say I could persuade him to tell me if ] put the matter tactfully."

Garland nodded. "Because if it is a fact, a reasonable motive seems to be established. You may say that Geoffrey benefits by his nephew's death to the extent that he becomes the owner of the Hithering property. But is that ownership particularly attractive to him? I don't see why it should be. He's got a very comfortable little business here which brings him in all he wants. You've seen his house, and you'll agree that his standard of living is as good as anybody's. He likes to potter about at Forstal Farm at the weekends. Anyone would say that he's got pretty well everything a man wants to make him contented."

"Including, of course, his sister," said Arnold encouragingly.

"Oh, I expect he's used to her by this time. This is what I was going to say: Why should Geoffrey plug his nephew in order to incur the trouble and responsibility of an estate a hundred miles away from here?"

"I shouldn't worry about the trouble and responsibility as long as I drew the income," Arnold remarked.

"I dare say. But you're not exactly in Geoffrey's position. As I've tried to point out to you, he is very well provided for as it is. Besides, as anyone who knows him will tell you, his business is more or less his hobby. I shouldn't think he'd give it up even for the sake of becoming a landed proprietor."

Garland paused and tapped the desk impressively with his pencil. "No, you'll never persuade me that Geoffrey murdered his nephew just for the sake of stepping into his shoes," he continued. "But if young Basil spent Saturday evening dunning him for the ten thousand pounds, that's an entirely different matter. However wealthy a man might be, he'd hate parting with ten thousand pounds, I should imagine. And, in the circumstances, Geoffrey couldn't very well refuse to pay up.

"I dare say he went to bed that night wondering how the devil he was going to dodge the issue. Then it occurred to him that if anything happened to Basil the problem would settle itself. He owed money to the estate; after Basil's death the estate would be his. It would be the simplest solution in the world. In fact, it seems to me that Geoffrey's motive positively sticks out a foot."

Arnold shook his head. "That's all very well, but we can't build up a prosecution on that foundation alone. We can only say, 'Here's Basil found dead in Geoffrey's house and here's a convincing motive for Geoffrey wanting him out of the way. What about it?' The defence would submit that until we could produce some proof that Geoffrey contrived his death, there was no case to put before the jury. And they'd certainly get away with it."

"Well, it's up to you," said Garland. "What's your next move?"

"It seems to me that I can't do very much more here for the moment. I'm inclined to go back to London and make an appointment to see Mr. Rustwick, the lawyer. While I'm there I might find out what's become of Pelling. Probably he knows quite a lot about his partner's affairs. And there's a third man I'd like to interview if I knew where to get hold of him."

"Who's that?" Garland asked.

"The driver of the van that was standing outside the house on Sunday morning," Arnold replied.

## CHAPTER SEVEN

N HIS ROOM at Scotland Yard that evening, Arnold spent a couple of hours studying his notes. At the end of this time he had produced a summary which read as follows:

Events at the master's house at Tenteridge on Sunday morning, February 20th.

7.30 a.m.—Mrs. Dukes and Hetty arrive. Van not visible.

8 o'clock a.m.—Mrs. Dukes calls Geoffrey Maplewood. Receives his message about Basil having the first bath.

8.02 a.m.—Mrs. Dukes gives the message to Basil.

8.20 a.m.—Basil goes to the bathroom. Shortly afterwards the bath water is heard running.

8.25 a.m.—Archie Pender passes the house and sees a van standing outside.

8.30 a.m.—Mrs. Dukes hears the van and sends Hetty out to look. Hetty actually sees the van. About the same time Mrs. Dukes hears the bath water turned off.

8.32 a.m.—A noise is heard by Geoffrey Maplewood, Mrs. Dukes and Hetty. Described variously, but probably the sound of Basil falling to the floor.

8.35 a.m.—The van is seen by Williams in the act of driving away from the house.

8.50 a.m.—Geoffrey Maplewood knocks on the bathroom door and gets no reply. This is confirmed by Mrs. Dukes.

8.55 a.m. Hetty goes for Reuben Dukes. Sees no sign of the van.

9:05 a.m.—Reuben Dukes arrived, breaks open the bathroom door and finds Basil's body.

9:06 a.m.—Hetty is again sent to the farm to call Dr. Prescott.

9.10 a.m.—Dr. Prescott receives the call.

9.20 a.m.—Dr. Prescott reaches the house. At this time the front door is found to be locked and bolted.

9.23 a.m.—Dr. Prescott examines the body.

Looking at this summary, it became clearer than ever that the van was standing outside the house at the time of Basil's death. But had this fact any particular significance? Had the driver of the van any connection with the crime? And if he had, how did he know that Basil was in the house on that particular Sunday morning? The only reasonable answer to this last question was that *Geoffrey* had told him.

That was just the rub. Whichever way Arnold turned, the path of detection led inevitably to Geoffrey Maplewood. One might suppose that, distrusting his own homicidal ability, he had employed an accomplice to assist him. But why in the name of sanity had the crime been committed when it was with Mrs. Dukes and Hetty in the house as witnesses? During the preceding night, Geoffrey and his nephew had been alone for at least ten hours. And in the small hours of the morning, the presence of the van would probably never have been noticed.

But the presence of an accomplice—or accomplices, for that matter, since two or three other people might have been hidden in the interior of the van—made the method of the crime no clearer. How could even a number of people under the watchful eyes of Mrs. Dukes and her daughter have given a healthy young man a fatal shock when he was locked in a room to which they had no means of access?

This was the problem which Arnold took home with him to sleep upon.

On his arrival at the Yard from Addleford on Monday afternoon, he made an appointment with Mr. Rustwick for the following morning. He arrived punctually at the lawyer's office and was shown into the presence of an elderly man with a shrewd but not unkindly face.

"Sit down, Inspector," said Mr. Rustwick. "You have come to see me concerning the death of Mr. Basil Maplewood. The fact that the police have interested themselves in the matter suggests certain inferences which may be drawn. But let me make it clear from the outset that my only knowledge of the matter is based upon certain information given to me by Geoffrey Maplewood on the telephone yesterday morning."

"Then I will give you the facts as I have ascertained them," Arnold replied. He proceeded to give the lawyer a brief account of the events of the previous Sunday morning.

Mr. Rustwick listened attentively. "Your description corresponds very closely with what Mr. Geoffrey Maplewood told me. Mr. Basil Maplewood's death appears utterly inexplicable. I have known him from birth, and I can assure you that he has never known a day's illness. And, as it happens, he had only recently passed a stiff medical examination with flying colours, previous to learning to fly with a view to qualifying as a pilot. I shall be very happy to give you any information you may require."

"That's very good of you, Mr. Rustwick," said Arnold. "You won't mind, I hope, if I ask you a series of questions? Mr. Basil Maplewood was the owner of considerable property, was he not?"

"He inherited the Hithering estate on his father's death. At that time he was a minor, and Mr. Geoffrey Maplewood and myself acted jointly as his guardians until he attained his majority last year."

"Who is next in succession to the estate?"

"Mr. Geoffrey Maplewood as his nearest surviving male relative."

"Is it a fact that Mr. Geoffrey Maplewood owes the estate a matter of seventeen thousand pounds?"

The lawyer's eyes widened. "It would interest me to know who told you that," he replied.

"I had the information from Miss Phoebe Maplewood," said Arnold.

"Miss Phoebe!" the lawyer exclaimed. "May I ask how she comes into the picture?"

"She drove to Addleford immediately she heard the news of her brother's death, for which, I may tell you in confidence, she believes her uncle responsible."

"Good heavens! She has sufficient restraint to keep her opinion to herself, I hope?"

"I'm not so sure. I did my best to persuade her to do so, but with what success I can't say."

The lawyer smiled faintly. "It is not always easy to curb the impulsiveness of youth. But to answer your question. Miss Phoebe's statement to you is, in substance, correct. During his brother's lifetime Geoffrey Maplewood borrowed first ten thousand pounds and later seven thousand pounds from the estate. His brother, who was the very soul of generosity, refused to accept a higher rate of interest than three per cent. Nor would he fix any time at which the loan should be repaid. 'It's all in the family,' he said to me when we discussed the matter. 'Geoffrey will pay the money back as soon as it suits him, you may be sure of that.' "

"I see," said Arnold. "Has Mr. Geoffrey Maplewood ever suggested the repayment of any part of this sum?"

"Not to my knowledge," Mr. Rustwick replied. "You will realize that the terms of the loan make it impossible for any pressure to be brought to bear on him."

"Is it a fact that Mr. Basil came to London last week to consult you on this very matter?"

"On this matter among others. The position was this: Miss Phoebe is engaged to be married to a young fellow named William Bingham, whose father has for many years been agent to the Hithering Court Estate. It was her brother's intention to give her ten thousand pounds as a wedding present. He asked for my advice as to the best means of approaching his uncle for the repayment of this sum to the estate. He seemed to think that I could exert some influence in that direction. I was very sorry that I had to disappoint him."

The lawyer paused, adjusted his glasses, coughed and then continued:

"The fact is, that I think it most unlikely that Mr. Geoffrey Maplewood would respond favourably to any suggestion that I might make. No ill-will exists between us, certainly not on my side. But whenever we have had occasion to meet, we have found cause for disagreement. I feel quite certain that had the suggestion of the repayment of the money come from me it would have been sufficient reason for Mr. Geoffrey Maplewood to have rejected it. My advice to Mr. Basil therefore was to see his uncle himself and—well, shall I say attempt measure of tactful persuasion."

"Uncle and nephew were on perfectly friendly terms, I suppose?"

"So far as I am aware. Their characters were very different—the older man's cold and calculating nature being in sharp contrast to his nephew's impulsive generosity. But they had a common interest, both being very keen on farming, and this brought them together."

"They spent several hours alone together at Tenteridge last Saturday evening. Do you think it likely that a quarrel developed during that time?"

"It rather depends on what you mean by a quarrel. It is quite likely that difference of opinion arose between them. But I cannot imagine any violent altercation, for instance. Mr. Geoffrey Maplewood, though he can be as obstinate as a mule, is not of a quarrelsome nature. If opposed, he takes refuge in a sullen silence. And I am quite certain that Mr. Basil would have remained at least polite to his uncle so long as he was under his roof."

"You are aware that Mr. Geoffrey Maplewood—or at all events his sister Miss Monica—is not exactly enthusiastic about Miss Phoebe's marriage?"

"I might have guessed it," the lawyer replied. "Miss Monica's enthusiasms are reserved for incurable idiots and such people as that. And her brother is liable to be influenced by her opinion. They would consider that their niece was marrying beneath her position. Well, perhaps she is, but that doesn't seem to matter very much in these democratic days. In my opinion, young Bingham is keen and hardworking and might go far with a little capital behind him. As I dare say you know, he means to buy a partnership in a house agent's business in London."

"No, I didn't know that," Arnold replied. "Then the ten thousand Miss Phoebe was to have had from her brother would have been useful in that direction?"

"It would," the lawyer commented dryly. "Young William's expectations are confined to a share of what his father has contrived to save out of his salary. How much that may be, I have, of course, no idea."

"Is there any obligation on Mr. Geoffrey Maplewood, as his nephew's heir, to give Miss Phoebe a sum of money on her marriage?"

"None whatever. Miss Phoebe, when she comes of age, will inherit a small sum left to her by her mother. But it will not amount to ten thousand pounds, or anything like it. The fact is, the prospects of the young couple are in no way improved by Mr. Basil's death."

"Whose prospects are improved?" Arnold asked quickly.

The lawyer looked at him severely over his glasses. "That is a question to which you must find your own answer, Inspector," he said. "And now perhaps you will allow me to remind you that the punctuality with which a lawyer keeps his appointments is of considerable value to his clients."

Arnold took the hint thus broadly conveyed, left the office and returned to Scotland Yard. Here he consulted the criminal records for particulars of the trial and conviction of Ernest Pelling. These he found to be much as Superintendent Garland had described them. The records further showed that Pelling had served his sentence in Maidstone Goal, and had been released early in 1936.

Having gathered this information, Arnold sent for Sergeant Dobbie, who was, in his own particular way, one of the most valuable members of the Criminal Investigation Department. Not that the Sergeant's detective abilities were in any way above the average. In fact, Sir Edric Conway, the Assistant Commissioner, had on a certain occasion recorded his opinion that Dobbie wouldn't detect the Atlantic until he fell into it. The Sergeant's value lay in quite a different direction. His rather slow-moving mind was a regular dictionary of criminal biography. And, in addition, he had an amazing memory for the faces of all the crooks he had ever seen.

"Sit down, Dobbie," said Arnold as the Sergeant entered his room. "Ernest Pelling, sentenced to three years at the Old Bailey in August, 1933. Can you tell me anything about him?"

Dobbie allowed the question time to sink in. "Yes, sir," he replied deliberately. "Young, rather good-looking chap. He was barely thirty at the time. Very clever, too. Had invented a new sort of paper, it was said, I remember; but not clever enough to forge his partner's signature on a cheque and get away with it."

"That's the man," said Arnold. "Pretty obvious case, wasn't it?"

Dobbie shrugged his shoulders. "He might as well have pleaded guilty and saved everybody time and trouble, sir. A child could have managed the forgery better than he did. He made a carbon paper tracing of his partner's signature and wrote over it in ink. Naturally, the expert chaps saw through that easily enough. Why, the actual piece of carbon he had used was found and produced in court."

"Do you happen to know what became of him after his release?"

Dobbie made a second profound effort of memory. "He was well enough off, sir, I remember that. His partner behaved very decently and bought him out of the business. Several thousand pounds he paid him, if my recollection serves. Pelling set up for himself a business, selling wireless sets and gramophones and all that, under the name of John Ernest. Somewhere in one of the newer suburbs it was. Let me think, now. Orpington, it was. Yes, that's right."

"Well, slip down to Orpington and see if he's still there. If he isn't, find out what's become of him. And ring me up from the police station as soon as you can."

Soon after Dobbie had departed on his errand, Arnold received a reply to a telegram he had sent out earlier in the day. The message was brief and to the point:

"SORRY IN BED WITH 'FLU. COUNT ME OUT.

"MERRION."

Arnold swore vividly and at creditable length. This was just the sort of case in which Merrion's imagination would have been invaluable. He had a way of looking at things peculiar to himself. He would get hold of some inconspicuous thread and worry at it until the whole skein disentangled itself. And now, just when his inspiration was most needed, he must be idling in bed gorging himself with bovril and milk or something equally wholesome. It really was exasperating.

The Inspector, feeling that fate was playing him a dirty trick, took himself out to lunch. A nicely done steak and a tankard of beer put him on rather better terms with himself. If Merrion wasn't available he would have to get on as best he could without him, and that was all there was about it. Now, how would Merrion have tackled the problem if it had been set before him?

Arnold lighted his pipe and began to postulate the answer to this question. First of all Merrion would have tried to find out all he could about the motive. Arnold congratulated himself that he had already done that. This was one of the cases in which the question of motive presented no difficulty whatever.

In fact Arnold, in a satisfied mood after his lunch, felt that he could already answer most of the questions which Merrion would have asked. What was the crime? The murder of Basil Maplewood. At least everything pointed to that unfortunate young man having been murdered. Who did it? Obviously his uncle, Geoffrey Maplewood. When was it done? No difficulty there. The time could be fixed almost to the minute: at half-past eight in the morning of Sunday, February 20th. Where was it done? Again no difficulty. In the bathroom of the master's house at Tenteridge. How was it done? That, unfortunately, was the one question to which no reasonable answer had yet been suggested. It was just the gap that Merrion's imagination could have helped to fill. Confound the man. Surely he could have arranged to have his attack of influenza at some more convenient time.

Only two questions remained: What was the motive of the crime? No need to go further into the obvious. Finally, were there any accomplices before or after the event? At present, there was some little doubt about that. The driver of the van might not have had a hand in the affair. Arnold felt quite certain of the innocence of both Mrs. Dukes and Hetty. He walked up to the Yard, and was still deep in thought when he reached his room. Shortly afterwards his meditations were interrupted by a telephone call.

"It's Dobbie, sir, speaking from Orpington Police Station. I found the shop all right. John Ernest written up over the door. Smartish place, too, with big windows and two or three slap-up girls serving inside. So I went in and asked one of the young ladies if she had a record called 'Come and be Looney Under the Moon.' It's one my daughter's always playing; and a lovely tune it is."

"I dare say it is," said Arnold impatiently. "Get on, man, for mercy's sake."

Dobbie replied without symptom of undue haste. "Well, sir, the girl looked round the shop and, as luck would have it, she couldn't find that particular record. So I made as if I was angry with her, poor thing. I said she'd been wasting my time and that I wanted to see the boss and tell him what I thought about it. She went out and fetched him, and as soon as he came in I recognized Ernest Pelling. He still looks just the same as he did that day he stood in the dock. He was very civil and said that he'd get the record for me in a couple of days, but I said that I could get it somewhere else, and walked out of the shop."

"He didn't recognize you, I suppose?"

"Oh no, sir, no fear of that. He never knew me properly, so to speak, although I knew him."

"All right, that will do for the present. I shall call on Pelling myself this afternoon. Tell me how to find his shop."

An hour or so later, Arnold caught a train from Charing Cross to Orpington. During the journey he was still wondering how Merrion would have tackled the problem. He wouldn't have set about it in any common-sense fashion. He never did that. His method was to work out some utterly fanciful theory and slog away at it until his infernal luck showed him the very clue he wanted. But no theory, however fanciful, could possibly be made to fit the present case.

Geoffrey Maplewood had bumped off his nephew, so much was perfectly obvious. The young fellow threatened to become a nuisance with his request for repayment of the money and was better out of the way. But how the devil had Geoffrey managed the job? Basil had died suddenly in a locked bathroom to which there was no possible means of access. Even assuming that his uncle had an accomplice—or a dozen accomplices, for that matter—the problem remained insoluble.

There was so little that one could use as a jumping-off stage. Only that message which Geoffrey had sent to his nephew by Mrs. Dukes. He was to have first use of the bathroom. But why hadn't all that been arranged overnight? One would have expected Geoffrey to have said as his nephew went up to bed, "Well, good night, old chap. You take the first bath in the morning, and don't be too long about it." Something like that. Why the necessity for the message in the morning?

Because the scheme hadn't been perfected when Basil went to bed. But he, a thoroughly healthy young man, had probably been a sound sleeper. Mrs. Dukes had had to rap twice on his bedroom door before she woke him. Once he had gone to bed, Geoffrey Maplewood had the rest of the night before him. How had he employed it?

In making his preparations, whatever they were. He had the run of the house, since his sleeping nephew was the only other occupant. He could easily have left the house, letting himself out by the front door and locking and bolting it behind him when he came back. In fact, during the interval between his nephew going to bed and the arrival of Mrs. Dukes and Hetty next morning, he could have done almost anything.

And then Arnold was struck with a sudden idea. Almost anything—especially if you had the assistance of an accomplice with a motor van.

The Inspector glanced again at his time-table. It could be taken for granted that the van was nowhere in sight at half-past seven on

Sunday morning. But it might have been hidden somewhere in the vicinity. The routine of the house was regular and invariable. Geoffrey Maplewood knew that Mrs. Dukes and her daughter would arrive at half-past seven, with a margin of unpunctuality of only a very few minutes. And he knew that once they were in the house they would be too busy to take much notice of a strange van stopping outside. Again, Geoffrey Maplewood as host would have the deciding voice as to what time his guest should go to bed.

These considerations opened up a wide range of possibilities. Let it be supposed that when he heard from his nephew of his intended visit, he guessed that it was not entirely concerned with the new harrow. He knew that Phoebe was to be married, and he probably guessed that her brother intended to present her with a sum of money on that occasion. It was highly probable that he would be asked to repay part of the money he had borrowed from the estate. And he decided that to save himself any such inconvenience he would quietly put his nephew out of the way.

And what an opportunity! On Saturday night he and his intended victim would be alone in the house for hours; and his ingenuity was sufficient for him to devise some method of murder which would not immediately be apparent. Never mind for a moment what it was. One could assume that the scheme involved the employment of a motor vehicle and its driver.

These were available. Geoffrey Maplewood got in touch with the driver and issued his instructions. The man was to come to the house at some specified time, at midnight, for the sake of argument, bringing something with him. Again, never mind what that something might have been. Having arrived, he was to wait outside until Geoffrey Maplewood joined him.

Everything went according to plan. Geoffrey Maplewood, having apparently retired for the night, came downstairs again and waited until he heard the van draw up. He went out, met the driver and took from him what he had brought. This he carried up to the bathroom. It was something that would prove fatal to anyone shut up in the same room with it.

Excellent so far. But at this point Arnold's imagination was pulled up short. Geoffrey Maplewood would have had no difficulty in introducing almost anything he liked into the bathroom. But how was he to remove it once its work was done? His nephew had locked the door behind him, and it had remained locked until Reuben Dukes had burst it open. And surely Dukes or his wife or daughter would have noticed any unfamiliar object in the room?

And then, for the second time within a few minutes, Arnold had an inspiration. The statement of young Will Owens riding past the house on his way to visit his girl. He had seen the van driver sitting in the driver's seat and apparently coiling up a rope. That trifling detail was the clue.

The object, whatever it was, had a rope, or more likely a stout cord, such as a blind cord, attached to it. When Geoffrey had placed it in position, he had thrown the other end of the cord through the window, across the shrubbery into the road. The accomplice had picked it up and hidden it behind the garden wall. He had then driven off to return at the appointed time next morning. Geoffrey would have estimated within a few minutes when his nephew would be in the bathroom.

When the van returned, the driver got out and pretended to occupy himself with the engine. But actually he was waiting for some signal given to him by Geoffrey from within the house. When the signal came he reached over the wall for the end of the cord and pulled on it, thus drawing the object out of the bathroom window and across the top of the shrubbery. When he had secured the object he put it in the van, coiled up the rope and drove away. As the train drew into Orpington Station, Arnold smiled knowingly. It was a lovely theory. Not Merrion himself with his powers of vivid imagination could have evolved a better one.

## CHAPTER EIGHT

F OLLOWING DOBBIE'S instructions, Arnold had no difficulty in locating the shop at Orpington. It had a flourishing, businesslike appearance, and half a dozen customers at least were present when the Inspector walked in. He waited until one of the girls had leisure to attend to him, then gave her a card enclosed in an envelope with a request that it might be given to Mr. Ernest.

The girl took the card and returned almost immediately. Arnold followed her into the private office, where he found himself confronted by a youngish-looking man, fair, clean-shaven and smartly-dressed, who asked him politely enough to sit down.

Arnold complied with the invitation but said nothing until the girl had left the room. And when he spoke it was in a quiet voice: "Your name is Ernest Pelling, I believe."

The other flushed angrily: "And what if it is?" he replied. "Am I to be pestered by the police to the end of my days?"

Arnold leant back in his chair and smiled. "My dear man, who's pestering you?" he replied. "I'm not even remotely interested in the forgotten past. I came to see you this afternoon to talk about your late partner, Mr. Geoffrey Maplewood."

At the mention of this name Pelling stiffened suddenly. "Geoffrey!" he exclaimed. "Why, what's happened to him?"

"Nothing's happened to him," said Arnold. "But his nephew, Mr. Basil Maplewood, died suddenly it the bathroom of his uncle's house at Tenteridge on Sunday morning."

For a moment or two Pelling stared at the Inspector with wide open eyes. Then suddenly he burst into hysterical laughter. "His nephew!" he spluttered. "Well, I'll be damned. Accidents will happen even in the best regulated families, they say. So young Basil's dead, is he? Then, unless I'm greatly mistaken, Geoffrey becomes the owner of Hithering Court, the family place?"

"So I am informed," Arnold replied shortly. "Now will you forgive me, Mr. Pelling, if I am compelled to revive painful memories? During your association with Geoffrey Maplewood you got on pretty well with him, didn't you?"

Pelling shrugged his shoulders. "We were never exactly bosom friends. Geoffrey was far too self-centred ever to be really friendly with anybody. But as you suggest, we got on well enough. As far as the business went, we pulled together all right. That old fox Geoffrey was in charge of the office, and I looked after the technical side."

"You used to spend week-ends with him at Tenteridge house, didn't you?"

Pelling nodded. "I did," he replied. "Not because I was particularly interested in the place or its surroundings, but because if Geoffrey and I wanted a quiet business talk it was the only refuge from the tongue of his sister. Have you met her, by any chance? Does she still prattle about that Institute of hers? If incurable imbecility is the only qualification, she should be an inmate herself."

"Yes, I've met Miss Maplewood," Arnold replied. "But it's her brother I want to talk about. You've been to this house at Tenteridge, you tell me. Did you see it before he had it altered?"

"Several times—at least half a dozen, I should think. Geoffrey asked my advice about putting in a bathroom and bringing the house up to date generally. I told him that I didn't know much about building, but that it wouldn't hurt him much to employ an architect to get out a scheme. But he wouldn't do that. He would never spend a penny more than he could possibly help. In the end he gave the job to a local builder, who carried it out after his awn fashion. His work was sound enough, I dare say, but it was hardly spectacular. Of course, Geoffrey may have had something else done by now. I haven't been near the place for five years or more."

"Have you met Mr. Geoffrey Maplewood during these five years?"

Pelling frowned slightly. "In the circumstances a meeting between us might have been a trifle awkward. On the other hand, I have indirectly been in touch with him. He made a certain offer which I accepted. I couldn't very well do anything else. But all the negotiations were carried out through a lawyer."

"Mr. Rustwick, the Maplewood family solicitor, perhaps?" Arnold suggested.

But Pelling shook his head vigorously. "Not on your life!" he replied. "Geoffrey had no use for him at any time. The truth is, Inspector, that Geoffrey had to borrow money from his brother to pay for his share of the paper mill, and from what he let drop at the time, I gathered that Mr. Rustwick tried to stiffen up the terms a bit. No, the lawyer in the case was Fletton, an Addleford man."

"Did you ever meet Mr. Basil Maplewood?"

"Once or twice when he was staying at Riverbank and Geoffrey brought him down to the mills. A very decent chap I always thought, with none of his uncle's vices. I couldn't begin to make you understand how sorry I am that he's dead. He died suddenly, you say. What did he die of?"

"The doctors haven't made up their minds yet. That's one of the reasons why I'm making inquiries."

Pelling nodded. "I understand," he said. "But would it be indiscreet to ask why your inquiries should have led you to me?"

There was an unmistakable note of resentment in his voice, and Arnold smiled disarmingly. "I told you just now that I wasn't faintly interested in the forgotten past. But ever since I have been on the case, your name kept cropping up as one who knew Geoffrey Maplewood and his affairs more intimately than most people. And I want you to tell me what you can about him."

"Without prejudice, I suppose," said Pelling ironically. "Hell, I'll try. Geoffrey is one of those people who is never satisfied with what he's got, but always wants something else to add to it. I don't mean that he's ambitious in any worthy sense of the word. Put it like this: if he's got five shillings to spend he can't be happy for regretting that it isn't six. Get me?"

"I get you," Arnold replied. "And he does his best to see that it is six next time, I suppose?"

"That's right. It's just what he worries and schemes for. But when he's got it, he's no happier, for then he begins to regret that it isn't seven. And so he goes on.

"It's just the same with his farm at Tenteridge. He always tells people that he runs it as a hobby, or because he's interested in farming. But I happen to know differently. The farm's got to show a profit at the end of the year, or the unfortunate Dukes hears all about it. I tell you, it's anything but a soft job being Geoffrey's bailiff."

"Would you describe him as a good business man?" Arnold asked.

Pelling smiled queerly. "His business methods excite my admiration," he replied. "I don't think there can be many other people with Geoffrey's ability to drive a hard bargain. If he can save a farthing in a hundred-pound deal, he gets a momentary glimpse of Heaven. On the other hand, he doesn't mind paying as long as he's certain that he is getting the last ounce of value for his money. Paying in the course of business, I mean; not merely spending money just for spending sake. That was never Geoffrey's way."

"I understand," said Arnold. "One would imagine that he was pretty well off."

Again Pelling shrugged his shoulders. "He ought to be. The mill was flourishing when—well, when I last had anything to do with it. And it ought to be just as flourishing now, since it has the monopoly of the manufacture of Hermatine, which, it may interest you to know, is an invention of my own."

"So I understand," said Arnold. "I wish you would tell me something of the relationship between Geoffrey Maplewood and his nephew."

Pelling looked him squarely in the face. "Look here, Inspector, what's the good of beating about the bush? It's perfectly clear to me that you suspect Geoffrey of having some hand in young Basil's death. And yet you expect me to tell you something which would enable you to subpoena me as a witness at a possible trial. You won't be offended, I hope, if I must emphatically refuse to do anything of the sort?"

Arnold misunderstood the reason for his vehemence. "Your sentiments of gratitude do you credit," he said. "But—"

"Gratitude!" Pelling interrupted him. "Oh, I see what you mean. Of course I'm grateful to Geoffrey for buying me out so generously. Convicted crooks have no right to expect any consideration, I know that. But that's not my objection to appearing in the witness-box. Can't you understand? I've had one experience of my evidence being misbelieved, and I don't want another. And now that I'm an old lag, branded as a forger and a liar forever, you don't suppose that my evidence would be accepted with any great faith, do you?"

The bitterness in the man's voice was so obviously heartfelt that Arnold was moved in spite of himself. "I think I understand how you feel about it, Mr. Pelling," he said. "Actually you don't want the past raked up. But won't you give me what information you can on my personal undertaking that your name shall not appear?"

"Well, I suppose I don't mind doing that," Pelling agreed slowly and hesitatingly. "But, to tell you the truth, I don't know much about the personal relationship between Geoffrey and young Basil. Whenever I saw them together, it seemed to me that Geoffrey liked his nephew well enough as an individual. It was his existence that he hated, if you understand what I mean."

"I'm afraid I don't, altogether," Arnold remarked.

"Well, I'll try to explain. Geoffrey used to talk to me about it so often in the old days that I ought to understand his point of view. I said just now that he was a good business man. So he is. But now I suppose he's got so used to the particular business in which he finds himself that he's pretty well reconciled to it. But I had a desperate time before I succeeded in persuading him that it would be a marvellous proposition for us to buy the Addle Paper Mill. That wasn't the sort of business that his heart was set on at all."

"What was in his mind, then?" Arnold asked,

"Hithering Court—that and nothing else. When he was a young man and his father was alive he lived there and pretty well ran the whole estate. His elder brother didn't seem to have any interest in the place. He was a decent enough fellow, but he had no use for the life of a country gentleman. His idea was going to intellectual plays and attending the meetings of the various learned societies to which he belonged. He was, I believe, a great authority upon the manners and customs of the Revilla Gigedo Islanders although, of course, he'd never been there."

"Indeed," said Arnold, whose geography was not exactly his strong point.

"That shows you the sort of chap he was. Far more interested in outlandish things and people than in his own estate and tenants. Geoffrey always resented the fact that his brother would inherit the estate and not himself. And even after Basil was born I think he always clung to the hope that something would happen to give him what he wanted.

"But it didn't, and Geoffrey grew into a disappointed man. I don't want you to think that his love for the place was sentimental or anything like that. He saw that the estate, properly managed, could be made to yield a thumping profit. I've said it before, and I'll say it again: Geoffrey is a jolly good business man. He has an elaborate scheme worked out to the minutest detail whereby every suitable square foot of the estate was to be built upon. The rest was to be intensely farmed with a view to supplying the inhabitants of the houses when they were built. Eggs, milk, poultry, vegetables, and all sorts of produce like that. And Geoffrey, living at the hub of this activity, would have been in his element. He has often told me what he would have done if things had been different. And now—"

"And now . . .?" Arnold repeated quietly.

Pelling turned to him with a wry smile. "And now Geoffrey will be able to realize his ambitions," he said. "It's a wonderful stroke of luck for him, for nobody would have expected a young man like Basil to pop off suddenly. Though no one suspected it, he must have had a weak heart all the time, I suppose."

"According to the doctors his heart was healthy enough," Arnold replied.

"And yet he died suddenly from no apparent cause," said Pelling thoughtfully. "In the bathroom at the Tenteridge house, I think you said? But, of course, it's no business of mine."

"It's everybody's business to try to help in solving the mystery," said Arnold.

"Well, I've had a scientific education. That's how I came to hit on the idea of Hermatine, I suppose. I've got quite a pretty little laboratory of my own here, though owing to the needs of my present business it's physical rather than chemical. I'll show it to you before you go. I amuse myself in there in my spare time experimenting with wireless waves. There's a lot more to be discovered in that direction yet. Have you ever thought of the possibility of employing cosmic radiation as a source of power, for instance? I suppose you haven't."

"I most certainly haven't," Arnold replied emphatically. "You were going to say—?"

"I'm sorry. Like most people when their pet hobby is brought out, I'm inclined to ride it. I was going to ask you if you'd ever thought of examining the drains."

The suggestion sounded strangely familiar. Of course, that ridiculous woman Monica Maplewood. Arnold became suddenly exasperated.

"The drains!" he exclaimed. "What nonsense are you talking? I know that if drains get out of order they make people ill. But they'd have to be in a damned bad state to cause death like this."

"They would indeed," Pelling replied soothingly. "But I wasn't suggesting that exactly. There was no main drainage at Tenteridge when I used to know the place."

"I don't suppose there is now," said Arnold shortly. "What's that got to do with it?"

"Nothing at all, probably. But where there's no main drain, the sewage of the house has got to be disposed of somehow. The usual plan is to provide a cesspit which collects the sewage and can if necessary be emptied at intervals. And that's the system that Geoffrey's got at Tenteridge—or it used to be."

"I haven't the remotest idea what you're driving at," Arnold exclaimed.

"Perhaps because you've never had much to do with cesspits. People who live in town are apt to take all these things for granted. But if you're going to dig a cesspit at all you may as well dig a decent-sized one. I dare say the cesspit at Geoffrey's house holds a matter of 3,000 gallons. Taking $6^1/_4$ gallons to a cubic foot, that works out at 480 cubic feet. Quite a decent-sized hole, when you come to think of it."

At last Arnold realized the other's meaning. "Where is this cesspit?" he demanded.

"Outside the back door beneath the paved yard. You'll find the cover let into the farther side of this from the house. If I wanted to throw anything away where it wouldn't be likely to be found, it's the first place I should think of."

Arnold considered this for a few moments. "Thanks, Mr. Pelling," he said. "I'm duly grateful for the hint. I've already wondered whether anything might have been thrown away. The thing that was responsible for Basil Maplewood's death, I mean. But I haven't the remotest idea what sort of thing to look for."

Pelling glanced at him shrewdly. "You've realized, I dare say, that Geoffrey is a pretty up-to-date farmer. Well, the modern farmer has to wage perpetual war against pests. He's always sprinkling his crops with something or other, and he uses some pretty powerful poisons in the process. I dare say you'd find enough stuff of different kinds at Forstal Farm to poison the whole parish."

This was not altogether a new idea to Arnold. "I've thought of the possibility of Basil having been poisoned by some sort of gas or other," he said. "But up to the present, at all events, the doctors insist that his death was due to shock."

Pelling smiled. "With all deference to medical opinion, I've always understood that some obscure poisons produce much the same effect as shock—arsine, for instance."

"Arsine? What's that?"

"Nasty, dangerous stuff. Fortunately, one doesn't often come across it. But among the things that farmers use is a chemical called arsenate of lead. It would be quite a simple matter to produce arsine from this. And a few whiffs of it introduced into a closed room, through a length of hose-pipe, for instance, would polish off the strongest man."

"Ah!" exclaimed Arnold. Pelling's carelessly spoken words unfolded a new and an attractive possibility. Through a hose-pipe! Was an ordinary rubber garden hose-pipe the explanation of the rope seen in possession of the van driver? "That's a queer idea of yours, Mr. Pelling," said the Inspector, "But would the average farmer know how to produce this poison gas you speak of?"

"The average farmer?" Pelling replied. "Probably not. He'd know what arsenic of lead was good or rather bad for, and how and when to use it. He wouldn't trouble his head about any further possibilities it might have. But Geoffrey as well as being a farmer is a paper maker. And a modern paper maker has to have an extensive knowledge of chemistry, I can assure you. And he's got to have some facilities for research. It took me several months of research before I found out the proper basis for Hermatine, for example. And of course I had to equip a laboratory for the purpose."

"Where is this laboratory?" Arnold asked.

"Why, at the mill. Where else? Geoffrey grumbled like anything at the cost of it, but the success of Hermatine fully justified that. The laboratory is sure to be still there, if you're interested in it. Someone's got to carry out periodical tests."

"Would it be possible to produce—what's the name of the stuff you've been telling me about—there?"

Pelling spelt out the word arsine and the Inspector wrote it down in his note book. "Would it be possible to produce arsine in the laboratory at the mill?" he continued.

"It would be perfectly possible to produce arsine there, or any one of a dozen other poisonous gases. Whoever did the job would, of course, have to observe certain precautions for his own safety."

"And could the stuff be carried out after it was made?"

"Easily enough, if it were pumped into a container of some kind. The inner tube of a motor car tire, for instance, would hold more than enough to poison a dozen people. But I shouldn't make any experiments in that direction, if I were you. Arsine is infernally dangerous stuff to play about with."

"Trust me for that," Arnold replied fervently. "I'm very grateful for what you've told me, Mr. Pelling. I hope I haven't wasted too much of your time?"

"Oh, that's all right," said Pelling heartily. "I'm afraid I was a trifle peevish when you first came in; but I think you understand why. Once a man's been in quod, the very sight of a policeman is apt to make him jumpy for the rest of his life. Come and see my laboratory before you go. It won't take you more than five minutes."

He led the way from the office into a large room fitted up as an electric laboratory. As Arnold stared in amazement at the collection of elaborate apparatus, Pelling smiled.

"You didn't expect to find all these gadgets in the back premises of a wireless shop, did you?" he asked. "The truth is, research is my hobby. Apart from the fact that it's fascinating in itself, there is always the chance of making some discovery that can be turned into hard cash. How about the transmitting of power without the use of cables, for instance? We're a very long way from that yet, but I haven't a doubt that we shall come to it some day."

"I shouldn't wonder," said Arnold vaguely. "You've got a fine place here, Mr. Pelling. Well, I suppose I must be getting back to town."

"I have your promise that I shan't be brought into this business in any way?" Pelling asked.

"Absolutely." And, after shaking hands, Arnold left for the station and caught a train to Charing Cross.

His conversation with Pelling had given him plenty to think about. It was curious that his original theory of a poisonous gas should have received support from a man with a scientific training. This stuff arsine fitted the bill exactly. Geoffrey Maplewood, as a farmer, could procure lead arsenate without suspicion. As a paper maker he had a laboratory at his disposal for the making of arsine from it. The gas could have been led into the bathroom through an ordinary garden hose. And it was, no doubt, this hose that Will Owens had seen the driver coiling up.

The more Arnold considered the matter, the more convinced he became that the van driver was the key to the mystery. The surest way to bring his guilt home to a criminal was through the accomplice, where such existed. Why had Geoffrey Maplewood employed an accomplice? Obviously to remove the evidence of the way the crime had been committed. But surely the technique had been unnecessarily clumsy? Why the hose-pipe and the conveyance outside in the road.

Arnold flattered himself that he could have worked out a far simpler method. He would have pumped the arsine into some easily portable container—a football bladder, for instance. This he would have taken to Tenteridge and hidden away until the moment for action came. The moment would have been when Basil went into the bathroom. Then he would have put the tube of the bladder through the keyhole and squeezed out the gas. The only trace of the crime would have been the empty bladder—surely an easy object to dispose of?

And this method would have avoided the measure of employing an accomplice.

Still, as the matter stood, everything pointed to there having been an accomplice. To suppose that a passing van, entirely unconnected with the affair, had happened to be standing outside the house at the very time of Basil's death, was to stretch the long arm of coincidence with a vengeance. The surest way to solve the problem was to find the van and its driver.

But Arnold knew from bitter experience the difficulty of tracing a vehicle, especially when nobody had had cause to notice it particularly. Even when an accurate description was available, the task was perplexing enough. Number plates might have been designed for the purpose of deception, so easy were they to change at short notice. It would not be a matter of many hours to fit an entirely new body to the chassis if preparation for the transformation had been made beforehand. Even a coat of quick-drying paint would entirely alter the appearance, especially on a fairly old van.

Arnold's first move on his return to London was to get in touch with Dr. Hallam. But the pathologist's report was disappointing.

"I've made a series of tests which I needn't describe in detail," he said. "As a result of these, I'm no nearer to being able to tell you the exact cause of Mr. Basil Maplewood's death. All the appearances, or, shall I say, the lack of them, point to death from shock. But there are, unfortunately, no means of telling how the shock came about."

"That's not exactly helpful, Doctor," Arnold replied. "Can't you give me any idea what sort of a shock it was?"

Dr. Hallam shrugged his shoulders. "You folk expect us scientists to be as infallible as the Pope," he said. "You won't stop to think of the limitations under which we have to work. Where there are definite post-mortem appearances, or where a substance like arsenic can be found in the body, we are usually able to come to a definite conclusion. But when, as in this case, nothing of the kind is to be found, you can't expect us to be other than vague and, if pressed, to take refuge in technicalities.

"Now, you're a painstaking detective with, I suppose, the average amount of common sense. If you find A weltering in his blood on the floor, and B standing over him with a carving knife in his hand, you have some grounds from which to draw a fairly safe conclusion. In the same way, if I find a body with an ounce or so of arsenic in the organs I have very little hesitation in advancing a theory of the cause of death. But if there are no clues whatsoever, any theory that either of us may form is apt to be misleading.

"Dr. Prescott, who, between ourselves, seems a pretty bright specimen of a country practitioner, told me that his first impression was that Basil Maplewood died of electric shock. Now it frequently happens that in the case of death from electricity there are no abnormal post-mortem signs. If the body had been found in the vicinity of a high tension cable, it would be reasonable to attribute death to electric shock. But even then, there would be no actual proof that this had been the case."

"As it happens, there is no source of electricity whatever within a quarter of a mile of the spot where the body was found," Arnold remarked.

"So I'm told. And even if there were, you'd have to explain how the dead man came in contact with it."

"That's just it," Arnold replied. And then all at once he remembered a remark of Pelling's unheeded at the time. "I say, Doctor!" he exclaimed. "Wouldn't it be possible to send an electric shock through the air like wireless?"

"That's a sufficiently alarming suggestion," Dr. Hallam replied. "But fortunately you can set your mind at rest on that point. Most certainly it isn't possible. Even if it were, how could you contrive to select your victim? Out of the four people in the house, why should this unfortunate young man alone have been affected?"

Arnold shook his head despondently. "I don't know," he said. And then after a pause he added: "I've heard that if a chap breathes a stuff called arsine it might look as if he'd died from shock."

"Arsine!" exclaimed the pathologist. "Who the dickens has been talking to you about arsine, I wonder? Whoever he is, I dare say he's right up to a point. But there's one very important thing he's overlooked."

"What's that?" Arnold asked.

"The fact that if the cause of death was inhaling arsine, traces of arsenic would inevitably be found in the respiratory organs."

"And you haven't found any in this case,"

"None whatever," the pathologist replied in a tone of complete finality.

## *CHAPTER NINE*

E VER SINCE Police Constable Terry had been stationed at Tenteridge, a matter of three years by now, his ambition had been to acquire promotion. Not necessarily for his own sake, for he knew well enough that the higher the rank one obtained, the more arduous one's duties became. But he had a definite object in life, which he and his wife had agreed upon when they first took to walking out together. He meant to retire when he became due for pension and take a quiet little country pub.

But Terry was a strict realist. A pub was desirable because it would provide a couple of gregarious turn of mind with unfailing company. But that was about all it would provide. The profits of a country innkeeper would yield by themselves only the most meagre of livings. But the possession of a comfortable pension would get over this difficulty. The pension of a police sergeant, for instance. Or even, if fortune smiled, that of an inspector. Only in his wildest dreams did Terry's imagination soar higher than that.

How was the promotion to be achieved? In the normal course of events, it was a desperately slow process. In an out-of-the-way place like Tenteridge one might wait for years for a chance of displaying one's merit and ability. Nothing more exciting than an occasional summons for keeping a dog without a licence ever seemed to happen. But now fate appeared to have cast opportunity in Terry's path. The Inspector from the Yard, who seemed a very decent chap, with no swank about him, had told him to make inquiries about the van which had been seen standing outside the master's house. He had succeeded in discovering two witnesses to its presence. Would it not be a brilliant feather in his cap if he would trace the van itself?

Inspired by this idea, he set to work on a definite plan of campaign. From all accounts, the van had been old and in an indifferent state of repair. The driver, it seemed, had had trouble with it when it was standing outside the house. A choked carburetor, he had said. Dirt in the petrol system, probably, which might cause a recurrence of the trouble at any time. It seemed more than likely that the van had broken down a second time not very far away, in which case some further trace of it might be obtained.

Working on this theory, Terry spent the greater part of his time, when not actually on duty, cycling about the country. He visited every garage, filling station and pub inquiring whether on Sunday morning anyone had seen a shabby and ancient Morris van, driven by a well-spoken man with a black mustache and a leather cap.

A vague enough description, certainly. The only factor in Terry's favour was that there were fewer commercial vehicles on the road on Sunday than on any other day of the week. Even so, for a long time his inquiries were fruitless. Nobody had seen such a van. Or if they had, they hadn't noticed the appearance of the driver. Apparently he hadn't stopped anywhere for petrol or repairs, or even for refreshment.

Late on Tuesday evening Terry decided to abandon his search for that day at least. He had reached an unfamiliar part of the country, a dozen miles or so on the London side of Tenteridge. It was dark and overcast and he could see the lights of the south-eastern suburbs reflected in the sky. He had a long ride home before him, and was due to relieve a colleague on duty at the house at midnight. Terry made up his mind that it was indeed high time to turn back. But just at that moment he caught sight of a brightly-lighted window by the roadside a hundred yards or so ahead. He rode on until he reached if and dismounted. Yes, his instinct had not deceived him. It was a small but cheerful-looking little pub standing at the entrance to a straggling village. Terry could just read the wording of the sign: "The Walnut Tree—Bunting's Fine Ales."

He propped his bicycle against the wall and pushed open the door and walked in.

A couple of electric lamps revealed a cosy interior with a bright fire burning on the hearth. Terry, who was in plain clothes, walked over to this, rubbing his hands. "None too warm this evening," he remarked at large.

There were two other occupants of the room. Behind the counter the landlord, a short, stocky individual with the typical jovial publican's face. Sitting on the bench a thin, melancholy man, a glass of beer beside him and his face buried in a newspaper. To Terry's remark the landlord replied, "Cold it is. You're right there." The other merely grunted, took a sip of his beer and turned to his perusal of the newspaper.

Terry walked up to the counter and ordered a pint of mild and bitter, his favourite beverage. The landlord, having drawn it, engaged him in a conversational gambit, "You often round these parts?"

"Can't say I am," Terry replied. "Maybe I've passed this door before, but this is the first time I've ever stepped in."

"There's many that call in once that come again the second time," said the landlord proudly. "You'd scarcely credit it with a little pub like this, but on Saturday or Sunday, in the middle of summer, folks come all the way from London just to try my best. They say they can't get anything like it where they come from."

"I can quite believe that," said Terry, who had formed no very high opinion of Bunting's Fine Ales. "How far do you make it from here to London?"

"A matter of five-and-twenty miles if you go the right way. Straight on through the village till you come to a turning on the right; but don't take that, or after a bit you'll find yourself back where you started. Keep on it till you come to the second turning, the best part of a mile farther on, and take that. And after a bit you'll find that you've come out on the main road from Addleford to London."

"I see. But I'm not thinking of going up there this evening. I've got to turn back the other way. The fact is that I'm on the track of a motor van that there's been some inquiries about."

The landlord nodded comprehendingly as he surveyed Terry's upstanding figure. "I thought maybe you was in the Force when you first came in," he said. "A motor van? What sort of a van might it be?"

"A shabby-looking old Morris with a two-letter number. It was seen about these parts early on Sunday morning."

"Well, I'm blessed!" exclaimed the landlord. "I thought from the first that there must be something queer about it." Then, raising his voice: "Do you hear that, Tom?"

The man by the fire raised his face above the edge of his paper. "Did I hear what?" he asked peevishly.

"Why, this gentleman's in the Police and asking about a shabby old Morris van with a two-letter number."

"Well, as you know well enough, I've got something of the kind cluttering up my yard at this very minute," the man addressed as Tom replied. "Your friend's welcome to take it away if he wants to, so long as he pays what's owing for storage." And with no further display of interest, he returned to his paper.

The landlord leant forward confidentially over the counter. "Tom Burlap keeps the filling station just opposite," he said in a stage whisper. "Chap left a van just like the one you're talking about with him on Sunday morning. Said he was coming back for it, but hasn't turned up yet. Maybe you'd like to speak with him about it?"

"I should; but it's dry work talking," Terry replied. "Draw Mr. Burlap another pint and one for yourself, landlord."

At the prospect of a second pint, Mr. Burlap brightened up perceptibly. He flung his newspaper on the floor and finished his beer at a gulp.

"You're asking about that old van," he said. "Well, I've been wondering if the chap who brought it stole it. It's likely he did, though it's hardly worth the trouble of stealing. Anyway, I shall be glad to see the back of it. I've little enough room in my yard at any time, and that old thing standing there doesn't improve matters. And trade's not so good I can afford to have it littering up my place for nothing."

"How did it come to be left there?" Terry asked.

"Why, it was like this," replied Mr. Burlap, raising his second pint. "Here's your very good health. A bloke came along with the van on Sunday morning just about half-past ten. I was cleaning up one of the pumps and heard it coming. It was kicking up such a racket that I looked up the road to see whatever it could be. And there was that old van plugging along as if it would conk out any moment. When the man got up level with the pumps, it stopped and the chap jumped out. His face was all covered with black oil and the leather coat he was wearing was all smothered in dirt. Anyone could tell that he'd been lying on the road under that old van of his. And that's just what he had been doing, as he told me himself. He said that he'd been the whole morning doing twenty miles or so, and that he couldn't get the old van to go any length at all."

"Could you describe the man?" Terry asked.

Mr. Burlap scratched his nose doubtfully. "Well, I don't know about that," he replied. "I didn't see much of his face, now I come to think of it. What with the dirt on it, he looked more like a sweep than anything else. But I know for a fact that he was short and dark-like and had a black moustache. He was wearing a ragged old leather coat and a leather cap, the sort that has flaps that come down over the ears. Oh, yes, and a pair of driving gloves. He didn't look any too smart, I can tell you that. But he spoke a lot better than he looked; almost like you'd expect a toff to speak."

Terry nodded. "That sounds like the chap I'm after," he said. "What happened then?"

"Well, he said he was fed up with trying to make the van go. He'd promised to drive it to his brother's place somewhere the other side of London—Brentford, I think he said. But he jolly well wasn't going to spend any more time on the job. And then he asked me if he could leave the van in my yard for awhile.

"I asked him how long he wanted to keep it there, and he said only for a matter of a few hours. He said that he'd got his push-bike in the van, and that he'd jump on that and get to his brother's place that way. His brother had a lorry, and they would slip over here in it and tow the van in. So I said he could run the van into the yard, but I told him that I'd have to charge him half a crown for putting it there. He said that would be all right, and drove the old crock into the yard and gave me the half-crown on the spot.

"The next thing he did was to open a door at the back of the van and get out a bike. There wasn't anything the matter with that. It looked to me pretty well new. After that he took out a biggish suitcase and tied it onto the carrier at the back of the bike with a length of stout cord. I watched him and wondered at the time what he'd been up to. The suitcase wasn't one of those flimsy things, but real leather and stout at that. And the cord looked for the world like someone's washing line. And after he'd got everything fixed, he said to me that he'd be back some time after dinner. Then he jumped on his bike and rode off down the village. And that's the last I've seen of him."

"He didn't tell you where he'd come from, I suppose?" Terry asked.

"No. All he said was that he'd been all the morning covering a matter of twenty miles, or so. And that wasn't surprising, either."

"The engine was all to pieces, I suppose?"

"No, I wouldn't say that. Those old Morrises are wonderful. They'd keep on slogging along pretty well forever. But it was like this: I waited all day Sunday for the man to come back, and on Monday morning I thought I'd see for myself what was the matter. The old van was only firing on three cylinders, I could tell that when the chap drove up. So I had a look and found that one of the plugs was dud. The chap couldn't have known much about motors or he'd have spotted at once what the trouble was. And he'd got a perfectly good spare plug in the tool box, for I tested it myself. It's there now, for that matter."

"If he'd only changed the plug, he could have got on without any trouble, then?" Terry suggested.

"Yes, that's right; and it beats me why he didn't. And now there's the van lumbering up my yard, and I don't so much as know the chap's name or where his brother's place is. And there's another five bob owing for the two days she's been standing there beyond the time he said. You can see it for yourself, if you like."

Terry accepted this offer with alacrity. He and Mr. Burlap left the Walnut Tree and walked across the road to the latter's yard. By the light of Terry's torch they examined the van together. It was a fifteen-hundredweight Morris van of uncertain age, with an enclosed body in a dilapidated condition. The number plates were DD7241, and the license, which was in perfect order, expired on March 31st.

Terry noted these particulars and then proceeded to take measures on his own. He arranged with Mr. Burlap that if the driver turned up to claim the van he was to be detained on some pretext while the local constable was sent for. Terry then sought out his colleague and explained the situation to him. This done, he rode straight back to Tenteridge, whence he telephoned the news of his discovery to Superintendent Garland.

So it was that Arnold, on his arrival at the Yard on Wednesday morning, received a telephone call from the Superintendent.

"I've got a bit of news for you," said the latter. "Terry's found a van which he says was the one which was seen outside the master's house on Sunday morning. I've got the number and I'm making inquiries about it. But as you know as well as I do, it's doubtful how far that will help us. Do you feel interested in Terry's find?"

"You bet I do," Arnold replied. "I'd like to see that van for myself. Where is it?"

"At a little place called Plaxted, not a long way from here. If you like to catch the next train down here, I'll have Lambert meet you at the station with the car. You can drive to Tenteridge, pick up Terry, and he'll take you over to Plaxted and show you where the van is. How will that suit your book?"

"Couldn't be better," Arnold exclaimed. "I'll see you later in the day, then, and we'll have a chat about this business. So-long."

A couple of hours later Arnold reached Tenteridge and called for Terry, who told him the story of his adventures of the previous evening.

"Jolly smart piece of work," said Arnold appreciatively. "I'll see that you'll get all the credit for this. Jump into the car and show us the way to this pub you talk about."

It took Lambert a little more than twenty minutes to cover the twelve miles between Tenteridge and the Walnut Tree.

"That's the van still standing in the yard, sir," said Terry as they came in sight of Mr. Burlap's establishment.

The proprietor of the filling station, in answer to Arnold's inquiries, declared that the driver had not yet come to claim his property. The Inspector then proceeded to examine the van inside and out with the utmost care. Panels and wings were dented and badly needed repainting. The windscreen was cracked. The bonnet did not fit properly into place. In fact, the whole appearance of the van suggested that it had seen hard service, and very little attention.

The only feature of the van that was not old and worn was in front of the driver's seat. Here the floorboards had been renewed, apparently quite recently, for they were comparatively clean. They had been cut roughly out of one-inch white deal and whoever had made them had not been too particular about the way they fitted. One of the boards had a couple of wide oblong slots cut through it:

The tires, though they had seen their best days, were still in sufficiently good condition, for their threads were recognizable. On the near back wheel was a Dunlop Fort. On the off a Michelin. On the near front wheel a Goodyear, and on the off another Dunlop.. The spare wheel was fitted with a Michelin so worn as to be practically smooth.

The tool box contained the remains of the usual set of tools, most of the items missing and a spare sparking plug. The jack was broken and the barrel of the tire pump so dented that the plunger refused to work. The number plates, rather to Arnold's astonishment, looked surprisingly genuine. They had obviously not been moved for a very long time, and they had certainly not been repainted. The petrol tank was about half full and the battery, though by no means fully charged, was in good working order.

At the Inspector's request, Mr. Burlap removed the defective sparking plug and put the spare one in its place. When this had been done, the engine started with comparatively little persuasion. Lambert drove the van up and down the road and reported that, apart from considerable wear, the mechanism seemed sound enough. "If she had a proper overhaul, sir, I dare say she'd last for several thousand miles yet," was his verdict.

The body of the van was absolutely empty and fairly clean. Its scratched and battered condition showed that it had been subjected to rough usage in the past. But Arnold, after examining it very closely, could find nothing to suggest what its latest load had been. And Mr. Burlap, who had watched the driver take out the bicycle and suitcase, declared at the time it contained nothing else.

"Well, that's that," said Arnold. "I wonder if the Superintendent has managed to trace the number yet? You're on the phone, I expect, Mr. Burlap?"

The proprietor of the village filling station replied in the affirmative, and Arnold rang up Superintendent Garland at Addleford. His answer was highly satisfactory. The index mark and registration number DD7241 had been assigned to a Morris van, the property of Mr. Harold Swanley, of the Garage, Woodcock Green.

"Woodcock Green, sir?" replied Lambert in answer to Arnold's inquiry. "It's on the main road between London and Addleford. It can't be more than five miles or so from here, across country. What do you say, Mr. Burlap?"

"Call it six and you won't be far wrong," Mr. Burlap replied. "Take the second turning on the right through the village. Keep on till you get to the main road and you can't miss it."

"Do you happen to know Mr. Swanley who keeps a garage there?" Arnold asked.

"Can't say that I know him, but I pass the place often enough. It stands by itself just on the left just before you get into Woodcock Green."

"Right, I'll pay him a visit and see what he can tell us. You'd better stop here, Terry, and keep an eye on the van. All right, Lambert, you know the way, I expect."

They had no difficulty in finding the garage, which turned out to be a corrugated iron erection beside the road, with a row of petrol pumps in front of it. At the side of the garage was an open space on which stood half a dozen cars and vans, bearing notices that they were for sale at varying prices. Arnold got out of the car and walked towards the door over which was described the word "office."

A middle-aged man with a pleasantly humorous face came out to meet him. "Petrol, sir?" he asked.

"Not at the moment, thanks," Arnold replied. "I've come to find Mr. Harold Swanley."

"Well, you've found him all right," said the other promptly. "That's me at your service. What can I have the pleasure of doing for you? Perhaps you'd like to come into the office?"

He led the way into a snug little room where Arnold introduced himself. "I believe you're the owner of a Morris van DD7241, aren't you, Mr. Swanley."

"I was, but I sold the old bus last Saturday afternoon," Mr. Swanley replied. "Nothing wrong about it, is there? I gave the licence book to the chap who bought her, and I sent the note to the County Council. That's quite in order, so far as I know."

"Perfectly," said Arnold. "It's not so much the van as the man who drove it that I'm interested in. How long had you owned the van?"

"A matter of eighteen months or so. I took her in part exchange from one of my customers. Since then I've used her for rough work, and she's never let me down, I'm bound to say that. But she was beginning to use a bit too much oil for my liking, so I put her outside there, with a notice on her that she was for sale."

"How long ago was this?"

"Only last week, and I didn't think she'd go so quick as she did. But last Saturday evening, just as it was getting dark, a chap came along on a push-bike. I happened to be out at the front filling up a car when I saw him jump off and walk up to that collection of old iron I've got outside there. So when I'd finished what I was doing I went up to him and asked if he was looking out for a good second-hand car. Mind you, I didn't really think that he wanted to buy anything. From the look of the clothes he was wearing, you wouldn't have thought that he had more than sixpence in his pocket.

"So I was a bit taken aback when he answered me in as pleasant a voice as you please that it wasn't a car he was looking for, but a light van. I asked him what sort of a van, and he said he didn't care so long as it had a closed body. And then he asked me if I knew Tenteridge."

"Oh, he asked you that, did he?" exclaimed Arnold in a tone of deep interest. "And what did you say?"

"I said that I knew the place well enough, but didn't know anyone living there, which is the truth. And then he told me that his name was Dukes and that his father was bailiff at Forstal Farm at Tenteridge, which belonged to Mr. Maplewood, who owns the Addle Paper Mill at Addleford."

"He volunteered all this information without being questioned?" Arnold asked.

"Yes. I didn't ask who he was, for I didn't very much care. And he went on to say that for the past couple of years he'd been driving a lorry for a firm at Brentford, but that all the time he'd been trying to find a job nearer home. Now he'd managed to scrape together a few pounds and was going to start a fish round in Tenteridge and the villages about. That was what he wanted the van for.

"Well, I thought the old Morris would suit him well enough, and we went out for a short run in her. After a bit of bargaining we fixed a price which was to include putting in a nearly new battery I happened to have by me. We filled up with petrol, pumped up the tires, and there she was all ready for the road. Then we came in here. The chap sat down in the very chair you're sitting in now and paid me the price in pound notes."

"Quite a satisfactory deal, in fact," Arnold suggested.

"Quite. The chap went off jolly well pleased with himself. And he'll find he's got a good enough bargain. I won't say the old bus looks any too smart. But she's in good running order, and she'll stagger round the lanes with his fish for a year or two yet."

Arnold smiled. "Somehow I don't think she will. What did this chap look like?"

"Well, I thought he looked a bit rough when I first saw him. He had a black untidy sort of moustache and he looked as if a good wash and a shave wouldn't do him any harm. But the fact is, I couldn't see very much of him, for he was wearing a leather cap with ear-flaps and a tattered leather coat. As to his age, I put it down somewhere between thirty and forty."

"He came on a bicycle, you say?"

"Yes, that's right. And he had rather a posh-looking suitcase tied on the back of it with a length of cord. And before he drove away, he put bike, suitcase and all inside the van."

"Did he give you his name and address?"

"Yes. I told him I should have to notify the County Council who I'd sold the van to. And he said that his name was George Dukes, and that if I gave the address of Forstal Farm, Tenteridge, that would be all right."

"As a matter of fact, it's all wrong," said Arnold. "I happen to know Reuben Dukes of Forstal Farm, and he hasn't got a son. And this chap, whoever he was, didn't keep the van very long. He left it at Plaxted on Sunday morning and hasn't been back for it since."

"Well, I'm dashed!" exclaimed Mr. Swanley. "What did he go and do a thing like that for?"

"Because he'd no further use for it, I suppose. Now, Mr. Swanley, I'm going to ask you to run over to Plaxted with me and identify the van."

"All right. I'll just tell my foreman that I've gone out for a bit, and then I'll come with you."

As soon as Mr. Swanley set eyes upon the vehicle standing in Burlap's yard he recognized it.

"That's her right enough!" he exclaimed. "Well, I never thought I'd see her again so soon."

"Was there a spare plug in the tool box when you sold her on Saturday?" asked Arnold.

"Not to my knowledge, but I wouldn't be certain one way or the other. To the best of my belief, there was only a few odd tools, and not a very bright lot at that."

"I see," said Arnold. "Now just have a look at the floorboards in front of the driver's seat."

Mr. Swanley complied with this request. "Hallo!" he exclaimed. "The chap's found time to put in a new set anyway. The old ones were a bit shaky, I'll admit. He's used the bit of board I gave him, I can see that."

"You gave him a bit of board? What did you do that for?"

"Because he asked me for it. But he didn't say anything about making a new set of floorboards out of it. He said he wanted a bit of clean wood to put inside the van to stand his fish baskets on. So I gave him a length of my new inch plank that happened to be standing in my garage."

After some further inspection of the van, Mr. Swanley gave it as his opinion that with the exception of the new floorboard it was in exactly the same condition as when it had left the garage; then, shaking his head over the mystery, he entered the police car for Lambert to drive him back to Woodcock Green.

Arnold arranged with Mr. Burlap to remove the van from his custody, paying him the five shillings he demanded. But then a slight difficulty occurred to him. Who was to drive the van away? Here Terry stepped into the breach. He was a competent driver and held a licence. If the Inspector liked, he thought that he could manage the van.

"Upon my word, Terry, you're invaluable," Arnold exclaimed. "You take the van slowly back to Tenteridge. You'd better ask Mr.

Dukes if he can park it in the cart shed for the present. I'll follow you up as soon as Lambert comes back."

While awaiting Lambert's return from Woodcock Green, Arnold lunched adequately off bread and cheese and beer at the Walnut Tree. The car arrived just as he had finished and he got into it.

"Where to now, sir?" Lambert asked.

"Forstal Farm," Arnold replied. "I dare say somebody will find you a bit of grub, won't they?"

Lambert grinned and reddened. "I dare say they will, sir," he replied.

## *CHAPTER TEN*

THAT AFTERNOON Arnold paraded the van at the farm for identification. Hetty Dukes, being on the spot, was the first to inspect it. But she, womanlike, was unable to give a definite opinion. It was very like the van she had seen standing outside the house on Sunday morning. But she couldn't be sure. You see, she'd only taken a quick look at it, and as soon as she had seen that it wasn't bringing anything to the house, she had gone in again. But if it wasn't the same van, it was exactly like it.

Archie Pender was the next on the scene. He walked solemnly twice round the van before committing himself. Then he delivered judgment. It was the van all right, he was quite sure of that. There couldn't be another one so shabby outside the breaker's yards. Besides, it was the same colour and the body was the same shape.

Will Owens, fetched by Lambert from Tenteridge, was still made definite. He recognised the van at very first sight. As he approached it he had noticed the cracked windscreen and a piece of sticking plaster with which it was held together. He was perfectly certain that it was the same van.

Arnold, having sought and obtained Mrs. Dukes' permission, sat down before the fire and filled his pipe. He had no doubts whatever that the van now standing in the cart shed was the one which had pulled up outside the house on Sunday morning. Apart from its quite satisfactory identification, the descriptions of the driver given by Burlap and Swanley corresponded with those of Pender and Owens.

Nor was there any longer much room for doubt that the van had some connection with the crime. Why else had the driver given Swanley a false name and address? Why he should have given that particular name and address was a matter which Arnold reserved for later consideration.

Before leaving London, Arnold had supplied himself with a map of the district. This he now laid out on the kitchen table and proceeded to study it. He found that anyone going by road from London to Tenteridge had the choice of half a dozen routes, all of much the same length. He would follow the main road from London to Addleford for twenty miles or so, then turn off to the right at any one of the three or four cross-roads. He would then find himself in a system of secondary roads and lanes and would thread his way through these as he pleased. As good a way as any would be to turn right after passing Swanley's garage at Woodcock Green, leaving Plaxted a couple of miles on his left, follow a road which led more or less directly to Tenteridge.

By this route the distance from Woodcock Green to Tenteridge was sixteen miles. Woodcock Green to Plaxted was six miles, and Plaxted to Tenteridge twelve miles. The shortest possible distance from London Bridge, from which the mile stones weie measured, was by road twenty-nine miles.

As he studied these figures, the significance of the van puzzled Arnold more than ever. And even more than that of the van, the significance of the driver. He had called himself George, so, until his true identity was discovered, he must be known by that name. What had induced him to buy the van and abandon it so few hours later?

George had first appeared at Mr. Swanley's garage at Woodcock Green just as it was getting dark on Saturday. Arnold remembered the saying that one should be able to see a gray goose at a furlong at six in the evening on St. Valentine's Day. According to that it must have been getting dark on Saturday, 19th February, soon after six. The negotiations and the trial run must have taken at least half an hour, probably longer. George couldn't have gone off with the van before seven o'clock at the earliest.

His next appearance was outside the house at half-past eight next morning, a time established on the statements of no fewer than three witnesses. As nearly as could be ascertained, the van was stationary for about ten minutes. Finally, George turns up at Plaxted, with the van firing on three cylinders, round about half-past ten on Sunday morning.

The first question was, how had George spent the time between seven o'clock on Saturday evening and half-past eight on Sunday morning? It was ridiculous to suppose that he had taken rather over thirteen hours to cover a matter of sixteen miles. A normally active snail could hardly have taken much longer. Besides, Terry had reported that he had averaged over twenty miles an hour on his journey from Plaxted.

The second question concerned George's drive from the house to Plaxted. In this case, it had apparently taken him two hours to cover a matter of twelve miles. Six miles an hour could hardly be described as dangerous driving, but it was better than the previous performance. And George's appearance when he reached Plaxted suggested that he had had considerable trouble with the van on the way.

It seemed then that the first question was the more important. The answer might well be that George had not driven direct from Plaxted to the house. During the night he had gone somewhere to fetch something. But what had he to get and where had he got it from? And how had he disposed of it when he had finished with it?

And then Arnold was struck with a sudden idea. When and where had George made a new set of floorboards out of the plank which Mr. Swanley had given him? And what had he done with the old set which he replaced with these?

The Inspector left the kitchen and went out into the yard. Terry was standing guard over the van, but Lambert was nowhere to be seen.

"Hallo, Terry, you're the very man I want," said Arnold. "Look here, you know this country pretty thoroughly. If you wanted to hide this van for the night somewhere about handy, where would you take it to?"

"Well, sir, there are plenty of lonely spots round about here, where nobody would be likely to find it, especially at this time of the year," Terry replied thoughtfully. "About the best of them would be Queen's Wood. There's a track that runs right through it, which was made years ago when they were timber-hauling, sir. Nobody ever uses it now, particularly at nights, for it doesn't lead anywhere."

"How far are those woods from here?"

"A matter of a couple of miles down the road away from the village, sir."

"What's the surface of this track you speak of like?"

"Quite soft, sir, for it lies on the clay and has never been met-alled. Anyone would have a job to get along it if there'd been any quantity of rain. But with the dry weather we've had, I dare say the van would take it well enough."

Arnold pointed to the tracks the wheels of the van had made on the surface of the yard. "There can't be many cars with that par-ticular assortment of tires," he said. "If we find a set of wheel tracks like that, we shall know what made them. I think we'll go and have a look at Queen's Wood, Terry. Where's Lambert?"

"I fancy he's round at the back, sir."

"Well, go and dig him out. And I'd have a fit of coughing while you are at it, if I were you."

Terry grinned and departed on his errand. In a couple of minutes he reappeared with Lambert, who came to attention in front of the Inspector and saluted.

"Oh, there you are," said Arnold cheerfully. "I hate to drag you away like this, but I want you to drive us to a place called Queen's Wood. Terry will show you the way."

The three of them got into the police car, and in less than five minutes had reached their destination. They pulled up by the side of the road where a rough and uneven drive led into the depths of a thick wood tangled with undergrowth. The surface of this drive was yellow clay, not saturated but moderately soft and plastic.

Even as Arnold jumped out of the car he caught sight of the wheel tracks of the van. There was no mistaking the patterns of the different tyres with which it was fitted. The Dunlop and the Michelin on the back wheels, the Goodyear and the Dunlop on the front. With a word to his subordinates to keep clear, Arnold bent down to examine the tracks more closely.

The first thing he discovered was that the van had been driven into the wood and then out again. The tracks of entry were perfectly well-marked and distinct. There was no difficulty in deciding which were the tracks of entry, owing to the Goodyear in front and the Dunlop in the rear being on the left-hand side. But curiously enough the tracks of exit were not nearly so distinct. They were only faintly marked and in places hardly distinguishable. Even where they crossed the tracks of entry, as they did in several places, they hardly obliterated them. The deep impressions could still be seen under the lighter ones.

This seemed to suggest that when the van had entered the wood it had been heavily laden, and that it had come out again light, having deposited its load. In which case the load, whatever it had been, might still be hidden in the wood. But before following the tracks up the ridge, Arnold made a further discovery. This was the faint but unmistakable impression of the wheels of a bicycle.

The Inspector, delighted with the success of the investigation, pointed this out to Terry and Lambert.

"Here's a splendid lesson in detection for you chaps," he said. "Have a look at the ground here and tell me what you see."

Terry was the first to answer. "The van was driven in here, sir."

"Yes, and out again, too," Lambert agreed. "Though I don't see why it made deep tracks going up and only shallow ones when it came out again."

"Think it over," said Arnold. "Now let's follow this ride into the wood. Keep your eyes on and your feet off the track as we go."

With the Inspector leading, they followed the ride which ran more or less straight for a couple of yards until it branched out into an extensive clearing. Here it was easy to follow the movements of the van. It had been driven into the centre of the clearing and had stood for some considerable time, judging by the pool of black oil which had collected. It had then been turned in a narrow circle and driven out of the clearing by the way in which it had come.

"There you are, Lambert," said Arnold, pointing to the tracks. "You see that these tracks are distinct and fairly deep as far as the place where the car stood. But after that, where it turned and went out again, they are so faint that in places you can hardly see them. What do you make of that?"

Lambert scratched his head for a few minutes in profound thought. "I've got it, sir!" he exclaimed at last. "The van came here loaded up and went out empty. And it must have been a pretty heavy load, too, to have made all that difference in the tracks."

"Right! Now it's your turn, Terry. What about the bicycle tracks?"

"They both start off in exactly the same place where the car stood, sir. You can't very well tell whether they're coming or going. But both sets seem to have made much the same impression. I can't see that one is more distinct than the other. And the pattern of the tire is the same in both. Fairly new Dunlops on each wheel."

"What does that suggest to you?"

"That both sets of tracks were made by the same machine, sir."

"And when were they made?"

"After the van was driven in here, sir, and before it was driven out again. You can tell that by the way they cross the wheel marks of the van."

"Good again. We seem to be learning quite a lot. Now if both those sets of tracks were made by the same machine, we might guess that somebody on a bicycle came to meet the driver of the van as he was waiting here and then went away again. Did you ever hear of Mr. Geoffrey Maplewood riding a bicycle?"

"Never, sir," replied Terry emphatically. "I've never known him use anything but his car."

"Well, then, let's have another guess. We know that George arrived at Woodcock Green on a bicycle. When he drove away he put his machine into the van. We also know that when he left the van at Plaxted, he took put a bicycle and rode away on it. The probability is, then, that it was in the van when it was driven in here. So that it is possible that instead of someone coming to see George, he rode off to call on someone. Now, let's get back to the load which the van had in it when it drove in here. You said it must have been a heavy load, Lambert. How heavy, do you suppose?"

"It's hard to say," Lambert replied. "But, judging from the difference in the impressions, the van must have been the best part of a ton lighter when it went out."

"In any case the load must have been more than a man could carry away on a bicycle in one journey?"

"Oh, yes, sir, a good deal more than that."

"Very well, then. If it wasn't carried away, it must still be here or hereabouts. Hidden in the undergrowth at the edge of this clearing, perhaps. Scout round, both of you, and see what you can find."

The two set off across the clearing. They had not gone many paces before they stopped with one accord and bent down. "There's something here, sir," said Lambert.

Arnold joined them, to find three old cracked and very oily strips of board lying on the ground.

"I know what they are all right," said Lambert "They're the old floorboards of the van which were in it before George cut out the new ones."

"And there's something else here," said Terry, who was kneeling on the grass. "There's a lot of sawdust and chips amongst the leaves. And here's the sawn-off end of the bit of plank."

"Let me have a look!" exclaimed Lambert. "My uncle's a carpenter, and I used to work in his shop before I joined the Force. Yes, that's right. The sawdust's pretty fine, like as it was cut with a pad-saw. And the chips are made by a brace and bit, I'll swear to that. He had a pad-saw with him and cut the planks to fit the floor of the van."

"What did he want the brace and bit for?" Terry demanded.

"Why, to cut those slots you can see in the new floor-board. He bored a couple of holes right through and then squared them up with the pad-saw. There's one thing I can't make out, though.

Why did he cut out the board in this particular spot instead of resting his work against the van to steady it?"

"I think I can tell you that," Arnold replied. "I don't see how he could have got here before half-past eight on Saturday evening at the earliest, and by that time it would be pitch dark. So he took his work where the lights from the car would shine on it. If you look at the plank you'll see that this spot was right in front of the car when it was standing. He probably turned his headlights on to see what he was doing. Now I'll ask you a question: What did he cut the slots in the floorboard for?"

"That's always done, sir," Lambert replied. "There wouldn't be any way of lifting the boards out else, so they always bore a hole in them so you can put your fingers through and lift them out that way. There's a hole in one of the boards of the old plank, sir."

"So I see, but it's a small round hole and not a big square slot. However, it's a matter of no importance to us if George chooses to indulge his hobby of carpentry. Carry on and see if you can find that load, whatever it was."

While the policeman searched the undergrowth, Arnold sat down on a convenient spot and lighted his pipe. Up to the present he had been highly successful in tracing George's actions. Though these actions might seem meaningless, there was always a chance that the essential clue to explain them would turn up at any moment.

He finished his pipe without a word from either Terry or Lambert. Impatiently he got up to assist in the search. Those fellows must be blind if they couldn't find traces of a load weighing somewhere in the neighbourhood of a ton. Even had it been sand and George had scattered it as widely as he could, it ought not be difficult to detect.

But a prolonged ransacking of the wood revealed nothing whatever that by any stretch of the imagination could be connected with George or the van. Arnold called off the search at last and the three of them returned disconsolately to the spot where the old floorboards lay.

"We'll take those with us, anyhow," said Arnold. "But I can't understand about that load. Nobody can have found it and taken it away since the van was here. The only way into this clearing is by that drive, and there are no tracks there more recent than those of the van. It beats me altogether."

These observations were accepted by his subordinates in a respectful silence, until Terry cleared his throat a trifle nervously.

"If you'll excuse me, sir," he said after some hesitation, "but I've been thinking."

"Damned dangerous pastime for a policeman," Arnold growled. "What have you been thinking about?"

"Why, sir, that Lambert may have been wrong after all about the van being loaded when it drove in here."

"Wrong!" exclaimed Lambert, stung into indignation by this slur upon his detective instincts. "What do you mean? You can't help seeing that one set of wheel marks is a lot deeper than the other. How could that happen unless the van came in with a load and came out light?"

"Well, it entered my head that there may be another reason," replied Terry stubbornly.

"Let's hear this reason for yours, Terry," said Arnold.

"It's like this, sir," Terry replied. "On Saturday afternoon, it was warm above the ordinary for the time of year. But after sunset it got a lot colder, and round about midnight it came on to freeze. And when I went out about seven on Sunday morning, there was quite a lot of ice on the butt at the back of my house."

"By jove, I believe you've hit the right nail on the head this time," Arnold exclaimed. "Go on, Lambert hasn't seen it yet."

"It seems to me, sir, that if the van came in while the ground was still soft, it would make pretty deep marks, even if it had no load on. And if it didn't go out again until the ground had hardened a bit, then the marks wouldn't be so deep."

"That's perfectly sound," said Arnold. "And the bicycle?"

"It seems to me that both the tracks had been made before the ground got properly hard, sir."

"And when do you propose that the ground did get properly hard?"

"Well, sir, it would keep soft under these trees longer than it would in the open. It would take several hours of frost before it got really hard. I dare say that wouldn't be before five or six o'clock on Sunday morning."

"Well, it's worth thinking about, anyhow," said Arnold. "All right, pick up those floorboards and let's get back to the farm. Perhaps Lambert will be able to persuade Mrs. Dukes to make us a cup of tea."

Mrs. Dukes needed no persuasion, but promptly invited them into the kitchen to share the family meal. When they had finished, Arnold told Lambert to try whether the set of floorboards they had found fitted the van. Experiment showed that they fitted perfectly. There was no doubt that these were indeed the original set.

"What beats me, sir, is this," said Lambert: "Why did George go to the trouble of cutting out a new set of boards? I won't say that these old ones are any too good, but there's nothing really very wrong with them. They're cracked here and there, but nothing to hurt. They would have served his turn all right, as far as I can see."

Arnold shrugged his shoulders. "Just a passion for carpentry, I suppose. How long would it have taken him to cut out the new set and make the slots in them?"

Lambert glanced at them with an expert eye. "It's a pretty rough job, sir; but, even so, he'd hardly have done it in less than an hour—especially as he had no proper bench to work at. And there's another thing I've just noticed, sir. There are four screw holes right alongside the slot. I don't know what he made those for, I'm sure. But then, very likely they were in the plank before he cut it up."

Arnold arranged that the van should continue to be housed in the cart shed for the present. He told Terry to make inquiries locally as to whether anyone had seen it in the neighbourhood on Saturday evening. Then he got into the police car and told Lambert to drive him to the police station at Addleford.

During the journey he tried to piece together the information he had gathered. But in spite of his efforts they refused to make an understandable pattern. George's actions, so far as they had been ascertained, were those of an irresponsible lunatic. Confound that fellow Merrion and his most untimely sickness! This was just the sort of situation where his fertile imagination would have been invaluable.

When he reached the police station Superintendent Garland greeted him with his usual warmth. "Glad to see you again, Inspector," he said. "Sit down and make yourself comfortable. Well, what luck?"

"I don't know," Arnold replied wearily. "Thanks to Terry, who's a remarkably smart chap, I've picked up a lot of clues, but they don't seem to lead anywhere. How are things this end?"

"No further developments of importance. The inquest was adjourned pending Hallam's report. Basil Maplewood's body was taken off in a motor hearse last night to Hithering Court. He was to be buried in the family vault there this afternoon, I understand. Geoffrey Maplewood and his sister went down there by train this morning. And presumably Miss Phoebe has gone back, too, for I haven't seen anything of her."

Arnold breathed a sigh of relief. "I'm glad they're all out of the way," he said. "Especially the women. They're always a confounded nuisance in a case like this. Well, I'm bound to confess that I haven't found an atom of definite proof against Geoffrey Maplewood, though his motive becomes clearer with every statement I get."

"Who have you seen?"

"Mr. Rustwick and Ernest Pelling. The lawyer was quite noncommittal, as you'd expect him to be. But he made it quite clear that Basil's object in coming here was to dun his uncle for the money he owes the estate."

"That's worth knowing, anyhow. And so you unearthed Pelling, did you? What's he doing now?"

"He calls himself Mr. Ernest and he has got a gramophone and wireless business at Orpington. And he seems to be doing pretty well, too, from what I can make out."

"Let's hope he's prospering by honest methods. So he's set up at Orpington, has he? It's not so very far away from here, but I suppose he's prepared to risk anyone he knows recognizing him. You talked to him about Geoffrey Maplewood, of course? Did he seem very bitter? After all, it was his partner who sent him to gaol."

"No, I found him quite reasonable. Naturally, he didn't care to talk about all that business. But he was quite ready to answer my questions about Geoffrey. And he told me something that seems to me significant."

"What was that?"

"He said that Geoffrey had always been bitterly jealous about the estate going to his brother and nephew instead of himself. I think I can understand now how he worked himself up to the pitch of murdering his nephew. I'll explain if you like."

"I wish you would," Garland replied. "Knowing Geoffrey Maplewood as I do, it seems inexplicable to me. I shouldn't have thought he'd have the guts to murder anyone."

"Well, to begin with, he was pretty well born with the idea, if you see what I mean. He was obviously more suited than his brother to inherit the estate, but he could never do so while his brother lived. And then when that brother married and had a son, Geoffrey's chances became, if possible, even more remote.

"This apparently was the great disappointment of his life. Pelling told me that he used to talk about it, and I dare say the grievance still rankled last Friday. And then he heard that his nephew was coming to see him.

"I think, in spite of his talk about disc harrows, whatever they may be, he had a pretty good idea of what young Basil was after. Phoebe was going to get married, and naturally he'd want to make some provision for her. And there was that debt to the estate. Repayment of this could not, apparently, be legally enforced. But, for all that, it would be very difficult for Geoffrey to refuse a direct request of his nephew.

"It must have struck Geoffrey more forcibly than ever that if some convenient accident were to happen to Basil, then both problems would be solved, satisfactorily and completely. He would obtain possession of Hithering Court, which no doubt he assured himself was only right and proper. And the necessity of forking out a large sum of money would disappear. I think you'll agree that it isn't such a very long step imagining such an accident to contriving it?"

"You're right there," answered the Superintendent thoughtfully. "I'm quite ready to believe that Geoffrey murdered his nephew. But I'm as far as ever from understanding how on earth he managed it."

## *CHAPTER ELEVEN*

A RNOLD EMPTIED his pipe out into the fireplace and refilled it with the greatest deliberation.

"I don't know," he replied; "and my great consolation is that the scientists don't know either. They keep on talking nonsense about shock, and I defy you or anyone else to lay your finger on anything in the house so shocking as to cause a healthy young man like Basil Maplewood to die instantaneously.

"No. I think we'll have to leave the question of how it was done to turn to the question of whether more than one person was concerned with it. And I think I can satisfy you that the answer is that Geoffrey Maplewood had an accomplice who, for the moment, it is convenient to call George."

"To quote the slogan of a well-known advertisement: Where's George?" the Superintendent asked.

"Again I don't know. I wish I did, for I feel quite certain that he could tell us, if not the whole story, enough of it for us to guess the rest. George appears like a comet, circles round the house, so to speak, and disappears again into the blue. Listen and I'll give you an account of my snooping since Lambert met me at the station this morning."

The Superintendent duly listened to Arnold's detailed account of his day's work. "You haven't done too badly," he said appreciatively.

"Up to a point, perhaps," Arnold replied. "But let's try to figure out what all this is about. Obviously the first question is: Has George and his van anything to do with the death of Basil Maplewood?"

"They were within a few feet of the spot when the accident took place?" Garland asked.

"Yes, but that might be pure coincidence. The van might have broken down outside the house at that particular moment, but for one statement made by George himself. He told Mr. Swanley, the garage keeper at Woodcock Green, that his name was George Dukes, that his father lived at Forstal Farm, and that he meant to start a fish round at Tenteridge.

"Now it puzzled me at first why he did this. But I think I see now. He was afraid that someone might see the van in the neighbourhood, recognize it and tell Mr. Swanley. That would have seemed odd if his story had been, shall we say, that he intended to hawk coals in Newcastle. As it was, Mr. Swanley could only say, 'That's all right. I sold him the van on Saturday afternoon and the matter would drop. But you'll never persuade me that the van broke down accidentally at a place which George had mentioned at random. And there's another thing. How did he come to know Dukes' name, or that he was bailiff at Forstal Farm? Only if he was already familiar with the locality, or if Geoffrey Maplewood had told him. As for his being familiar with the locality, I would point out that neither Pender nor Owens recognized him, and they have lived in or about Tenteridge all their lives."

Garland nodded. "I'm with you hand in glove so far," he said. "Carry on."

"The next thing is to reconstruct George's movements between his appearance and disappearance. Now I'm quite satisfied that when George took the van over it was in sufficiently good running order. I don't think there's any question of his having been delayed anywhere by mechanical trouble. And it's my belief that he drove straight from Woodcock Green to Queen's Wood, taking not more than an hour or so over the journey. It was dark when he started, and darker still when he arrived. There wouldn't be very much risk of anyone who happened to see him or the van recognizing either subsequently. For the sake of argument, we can put the time of his arrival at Queen's Wood at half-past eight. Once in the clearing, he was to all intents and purposes safe from discovery as long as he laid low. But if he started sawing up planks or turning on the lights of his van, some passerby on the road might have seen or heard him. Curiosity might have induced the stranger to enter the woods to investigate. Had the invaluable Terry, for instance, been passing that way he would certainly have done so.

"That's why I think George didn't venture to make any move until midnight or thereabouts. What did he do then? He jumped onto his bicycle and rode out of the wood. We don't know where he went, but I think I can venture on a guess. He rode to the house to meet Geoffrey Maplewood—by appointment, of course. And he went on his bicycle because a bicycle is a much less conspicuous object than a van, especially such a noisy one as this is."

"Do you suppose that he took anything with him on this particular journey?" the Superintendent asked.

"I'm coming to that later. George, having paid his visit to the house, returned to the clearing. By this time it was past midnight, and there was very little chance of anyone coming along the road; so he turned on the lights of the van and proceeded to cut himself out a new set of floorboards.

"But that, I must confess, is where he beats me entirely. Lambert says, and I can see for myself, that the old set was in quite reasonable condition. Did George make a new set just by way of filling in time and keeping himself warm? No, most certainly he didn't. He particularly asked Swanley for a piece of plank, and he must have brought the tools with him in his suitcase, for I'm certain he didn't buy them anywhere after he'd left Woodcock Green. In other words, he must have intended to make that set of floorboards before he ever set out on his expedition."

"That sounds ridiculous," the Superintendent replied.

"I know it does. But there's something even more ridiculous that I shall come to presently. I told you how Terry accounted for the difference in the depths of the wheel track. If he is right—and I am pretty well certain that he is—we know that the van didn't leave the wood until the ground was frozen nearly hard, which Terry estimates at about four o'clock on Sunday morning at the earliest. Nor did George leave the wood again on his bicycle. It's my belief that he stayed approximately where he was until after eight, when it was time to start in the van for the house. Then he drove there, staged his breakdown and, after ten minutes or so, moved on.

"A couple of hours later he turns up at Plaxted, with the engine not functioning properly owing to a defective plug. He had a sound plug in the tool box of the van, but he made no attempt to use it. And, curiously enough, Swanley is pretty sure that there was no spare plug on the van when it left his premises. I think it's pretty certain that what happened was this: George brought a defective plug with him. At some time on Sunday morning, between the house and Plaxted, he took one of the plugs out of the engine, put this in the tool box, and replaced by the dud, thereby limping to his destination on three cylinders."

"But why should he—or anyone else for that matter, prefer to travel on three cylinders rather than four?" Garland asked.

"George's idea was to provide himself with a rational excuse for abandoning the van. He didn't care to leave it by the roadside, for the first cop who passed would take particulars and make inquiries. So he drove it to Mr. Burlap's yard. Remember, he didn't suggest that Burlap should diagnose the cause of the suggest that Burlap should diagnose the cause of the trouble. He merely said that he was fed-up with the van and that he'd come back later and tow the blessed thing away. And it's a fact that if it hadn't been for Terry's efforts it would have stayed there for days—not to say weeks—before any notice was taken of it."

The Superintendent nodded. "Yes, that's all right. What next?"

"Next comes the most ridiculous thing about the whole business. I think that it is fairly certain that George called nowhere except at the house from the time that he bought the van at Woodcock Green till the time he abandoned it at Plaxted. If he had, Terry is almost certain to have had news of him in the course of his inquiries. We know that George brought a suitcase and took it away with him when he disappeared. We also know that the suitcase must have contained, among other things, a pad-saw, a brace and bit, and a dud sparking plug.

"I'm quite satisfied that while the van was standing outside the house on Sunday morning, nothing was carried from it to the house or from the house to it. This would have been quite impossible, with Mrs. Dukes and her daughter running about all over the place. On the other hand, it is reasonable to suppose that George visited the house round about midnight. He may then have brought something or taken something away. But, whatever it was, it must have been capable of being carried on a bicycle. Do you see what I'm getting at?"

"Not altogether," Garland replied.

"Why, just this!" Arnold exclaimed, bringing his fist down on the desk in front of him with a resounding crash. "What was the van for? That's what I want to know. It brought nothing to the house and it took nothing away. Did George buy is simply for the purpose of sleeping in it during his night in Queen's Wood or of amusing himself by fitting it with a new set of floorboards? Of course he didn't. In any case, the van seems utterly meaningless. George could have done this business equally well, or better, one would have thought, on his bicycle."

"Perhaps when you've laid hands on George he'll be able to explain," Garland remarked.

"Lay hands on him! Yes, I know. But that isn't going to be so easy. He appears and disappears, and that's all we know about him. Youngish chap, dark hair and moustache, of apparently slovenly habits, yet nicely spoken. That's all I know about him. The slovenly habits may have been assumed, the moustache may have been false, or it may have been shaven off by this time. Not a lot to go upon, you'll admit. No, it seems to me that we shall have to set about looking for George in an indirect way. I think we've got to ask ourselves who Geoffrey Maplewood was likely to choose as an accomplice."

The Superintendent shrugged his shoulders. "Well, I can't tell you that," he replied. "But as we both know well enough, there are plenty of folks drifting about the underworld who would assist in any crime for a sufficient reward."

"That's true enough. But how would Geoffrey have set about looking for this man? He doesn't seem to be the sort of chap to be personally acquainted with the underworld. And he couldn't very well put an advertisement in the papers: 'Wanted, capable and efficient crook to assist projected murder. Highest terms offered and complete safety guaranteed. Apply Geoffrey Maplewood, Riverbank, Addleford.' "

The Superintendent laughed. "No, he couldn't do that. And I agree that he isn't the sort of person to associate with crooks."

Arnold leant forward and tapped Garland's knee significantly. "But for quite a long time he did associate with a crook," he said. "Look here, put yourself in his place for a moment. You have decided to murder your nephew. You have hit on a method which, for some reason we haven't yet fathomed, requires an accomplice. You rack your brains where to find him. And then you remember the existence of your former partner who has—well, shall we say, a criminal history. Eh?"

"Pelling!" exclaimed Garland. "You said just now that he was doing very well in this new business of his. He'd never run the risk of murdering a man he scarcely knew just for the sake of obliging his former partner."

"Possibly not, if it were merely a matter of obliging him. But you don't know what Geoffrey Maplewood may have promised or threatened, for that matter. And once a man has been put over the wall for a stretch, he doesn't look at crime quite like other people.

"Now, here's a theory for you: on Friday morning Geoffrey Maplewood learnt that his nephew was wanting to stay with him for the weekend. I'm not going to suggest that in a flash of genius he sees both the opportunity and the method. The opportunity, perhaps, but he must have had the method worked out long before. He gets in touch with Pelling some time between then and Saturday afternoon. How, exactly, I don't know. It isn't exactly the kind of subject one would care to discuss over the telephone, for instance. Perhaps he paid him a personal visit. Anyhow, get in touch with

with him he did, and they fixed the thing up between them. Pelling dyes his hair, puts on a false moustache, smears himself with oil, and there's George for you."

The Superintendent looked rather doubtful. "Well, what are you going to do about it?" he asked.

"I'm going to see Pelling again tomorrow morning. You said that Orpington wasn't very far from here, and I dare say Lambert can drive me there. I'll ask Pelling where he was at half-past eight on Sunday morning and several other questions besides. Meanwhile you might make a few inquiries about Geoffrey Maplewood. How did he spend his time between Friday morning and Saturday afternoon when he met his nephew? You see the idea, of course?"

"Yes, I see the idea," replied the Superintendent, without very much enthusiasm. "But you don't really believe that the man you call George was actually Pelling?"

"I shan't believe it until I have some proof. We haven't at the moment the slightest clue to the identity of George. He might be any one of at least half a million people. But it is pretty obvious, I think, that he was in some way connected with the death of Basil Maplewood.

"Now, so far as we have been able to discover, only one person in the world had any motive for murdering that young man. Nobody but Geoffrey Maplewood derives the slightest benefit from his death. George, therefore, must have been his accomplice. And it seems to me that the most likely accomplice for him to select is Pelling. That's logic, isn't it?"

"Yes, I suppose it is," the Superintendent admitted. "And yet somehow it seems to me that there might be a flaw in the argument somewhere. Disregarding the question of motive for the moment, what if George was playing off his own bat without any consideration for the feelings of the bereaved uncle?"

Arnold shook his head. "It won't do," he replied. "How could anyone have killed Basil Maplewood in that locked bathroom without so much as entering the house? If George had been seen hovering round the bathroom window in an aeroplane and a bullet had been found in the body, things might be different. But as it is, George must have entered the house when he rode there on his bicycle during the night, and had communication with someone inside it. And that someone can only have been ,Geoffrey Maplewood, as the facts of the case show."

"So that if you had proof that George was not acting in collusion with Geoffrey Maplewood, you would be satisfied that he had nothing to do with the crime?"

"If I had proof—yes. I should be compelled to believe several things about George. That he was one of Miss Maplewood's incurable imbeciles, to begin with. That his adventures with the van were part of some hoax of which I fail to see the point, that he gave the name George Dukes merely to mystify the excellent Swanley. Oh, and a lot of other things besides. In other words, if George was not in league with Geoffrey Maplewood, his actions simply don't make sense."

The Superintendent smiled. "According to you, they don't make sense as it is," he replied softly. 'You told me yourself that you can't understand what he wanted the van for."

"Yes, that's right," Arnold repeated. "Why was the van standing outside the house at the time of Basil Maplewood's death?"

"I've got an idea about that, and you're welcome to it for what it's worth," Garland replied, "You believe that George visited the house during the night and saw Geoffrey. I agree with you and think that all the preparations for the murder were made then. What they were I won't pretend to guess, but their success depended upon Basil being the next person to enter the bathroom. His uncle, as we know, contrived that.

"My idea is that the apparent breakdown of the van outside the house that morning was for the purpose of distracting attention from something else. A sound of some kind, probably. We know that George kept the engine running for at least part of the time he was there. This attracted the attention of Mrs. Dukes and her daughter. Hetty actually left the house to see what was happening. Perhaps the noise of the engine running drowned some other sound which might have given the clue."

"There may be something in that," Arnold conceded rather grudgingly. "But what sound? In spite of the noise outside, everybody in the house seems to have heard the thud of Basil falling to the floor." "Oh, probably some fainter sound than that. Perhaps a click or a pop, or something of that sort."

"Which brings us back to the method," said Arnold wearily. "Confound those doctors! They haven't been the slightest help to us. Hallam practically admitted today that he didn't know how Basil was killed. If this and if that and if the other he could have explained it, but all these ifs made it impossible. Look here, let's face the problem once more and see if there's a ray of light anywhere. Basil is found dead in a locked bathroom to which there are no possible means of entry. The window is open a few inches, but it is too small for anything but a cat to get through, and it is not overlooked from anywhere. Unless an occupant was standing against it, he could not be seen through the window, and everything suggests that Basil was not at the window but was getting into his bath when he was killed.

"When the door was broken open, three independent witnesses had a clear and an unobstructed view of the bathroom. Of these three, Mrs. Dukes and her daughter were perfectly familiar with every detail of it, since they were employed by Geoffrey Maplewood to look after the house. Yet they saw nothing unusual about it. It is, I think, quite fair to assume that at that time there was nothing in the bathroom which could have caused Basil Maplewood's death. And yet there was the poor chap as dead as a doornail."

"It is a teaser and no mistake," said the Superintendent. "There's no doubt, I suppose, that he died just as he was getting into the bath?"

"There can't be from the position in which the body was found. The same independent witnesses saw that."

"I don't know whether it's possible, but could anything have been put into the water to make it deadly?"

"Hallam took a sample of the water found in the bath for analysis. I got the report just before I left London this morning. The sample consisted of ordinary moderately hard water, containing no solid substance either in solution or in suspension. Incidentally, there was no trace of soap in it, which bears out the theory that Basil was only just getting in. As to where the water came from, I found when I was there that the company's water is laid on to the house."

Garland laughed. "I'm at the end of my suggestions," he said. "Come along and let's get something to eat. And if you insist upon it, Lambert can drive you over to Orpington to see Pelling in the morning."

## CHAPTER TWELVE

ON FURTHER REFLECTION that night, Arnold decided to stick to his plan. It was not that he was over-sanguine of identifying Pelling with the driver of the van. But the only chance of success in a case like this was to cast round in the widest possible circles. And, after all, Pelling had once been convicted of a felony, a fact which necessarily concentrated attention upon him.

So next morning Arnold found himself once more in Pelling's office. Mr. Ernest, as he now called himself, looked at him with scarcely veiled surprise. "Another visit so soon, Inspector?" he said. "What can I have the pleasure of doing for you this time?"

"I want to ask you a few questions, and I hope you'll be good enough to answer them," replied Arnold sternly.

"I'll do my best," said Pelling with a faint smile. "You want some information about my late partner, I suppose?"

"I want some information about yourself. To begin with, do you ride a bicycle?"

Pelling raised his eyebrows. "As it happens, I do," he replied. "I'm apt to spend too much time in pottering about my laboratory, so I bought myself a bicycle so I can go out and take exercise. I don't love cycling for its own sake, but at least it's preferable to walking."

"Where is your bicycle at this moment?"

"In a shed in the yard at the back. Would you like to see it?"

"Not at present thanks. When did you last use it?"

"I haven't used it this week at all. The last time I went out was on Saturday afternoon. We close early that day, and I am more or less free after lunch. So I took out the bicycle and rode to Westerham and back."

"What time was this?"

"I couldn't say exactly. But it was dark when I got home. Between six and seven, I should imagine."

"Where did you spend the night?"

"Why, here, of course. I've hardly spent a night away from home since I bought this business. I didn't leave the premises again until Sunday afternoon, when I went for a short walk. No farther than from here to the pillar box at the corner to post some letters."

"Who did you see between Saturday and Sunday afternoon?"

Pelling frowned. "I saw nobody," he replied. "Who do you expect me to see? A man in my position, if he is at all sensitive, is very careful to avoid making friends or even acquaintances. People are so damnably apt to be inquisitive about one's past. And naturally I'm not anxious for the news to get round this town that the retiring Mr. Ernest is really the ex-convict, Pelling. That's one reason why I spend the greater part of my spare time in the laboratory, where at least I'm safe from intrusion."

Arnold almost disregarded the bitterness in the other's words. "You say you saw nobody during that period. Did anyone see you? Can you produce a single witness to say where you were at half-past eight on Sunday morning?"

This time Pelling smiled. "No, Inspector, I can't," he replied quietly. "You'll forgive me if I read your thoughts, I know. You suspect me of having had a hand in the death of that poor fellow, which I honestly assure you no one regrets more than I do. Isn't that it?"

"There is reason to believe that some person not yet identified was implicated," said Arnold, evading the direct question.

"So naturally the ex-convict falls under suspicion. But can you suggest any possible motive that I might have had for killing Basil Maplewood?"

"That's not the point," said Arnold roughly, seeing the justice of Pelling's remarks. "You say you can produce no witness as to your whereabouts on Sunday morning? Where do you live? Don't you keep somebody to wait on you?"

"I live in comparative comfort over this shop," Pelling replied. "You're welcome to inspect my rooms whenever you like. And I employ a worthy woman who rejoices in the name of Mrs. Bullis, who comes in for a couple of hours in the mornings to clean up and an hour in the evenings to cook my dinner. But she doesn't come in on Saturday evenings or at all on Sundays."

"How do you manage about your meals at the week-ends, then?" Arnold demanded.

"How do you suppose I manage? I cook them myself, of course. Why must it always be supposed that no man unless he's a professional chef can. so much as boil an egg without turning it into a stone in the process? Cooking is only a branch of chemistry after all, and as I think I have already told you, I pride myself upon at least a nodding acquaintance with that science. I'll admit that now and again I go up to London on Saturday evenings for dinner and a show, but I didn't last Saturday."

"How did you spend your time, then?"

"After I came back from my ride I set to work to cook the dinner that Mrs. Bullis had prepared for me. It consisted, I remember, of a fried fillet of plaice, a roast loin of lamb and angels on horseback. When I had cooked, eaten and cleared this away, I went into the laboratory, where I worked till close on midnight. After that I went to bed and had an averagely good night. Sunday morning I spent writing a few letters—three, to be exact—and doing a few odd jobs about the house. For lunch—"

"Oh, never mind that," exclaimed Arnold impatiently. "I don't care a damn what you had to eat. I want you to produce some convincing evidence that you were here early on Sunday morning."

Pelling spread out his hands in a deprecating gesture. "My dear man, that's just what I can't do," he replied. "As I've already explained, I can't produce the vestige of an alibi. I can't prove that I wasn't at Tenteridge early on Sunday morning. But, equally, you can't prove that I was. And before you accuse me of the crime, at least suggest a motive that drove me to commit it."

Arnold shied away from this. "When did you last see Geoffrey Maplewood?" he asked.

"When he stood in the witness-box at my trial," Pelling replied equably. "I have not seen him since nor have I had any direct communication with him. As I think I told you before, our subsequent negotiations were conducted through a solicitor."

"Do you mean to tell me that you neither saw nor communicated with him on Friday or Saturday last?"

"You would think the word of honor of an ex-convict a mere waste of breath," Pelling replied solemnly. "I can only assure you that for a very long time now I have not seen or spoken to him or received any message or communication from him whatever, and you can confirm that statement, at least, easily enough. You've only got to ask Geoffrey himself."

"And he'd say the same thing, no doubt. You greed upon that beforehand."

Pelling stared at Arnold for a moment and then laughed outright. "Sorry, Inspector," he said apologetically. "I see what's in your mind now, and I can't help being amused at it. Geoffrey hired me to murder his nephew—isn't that it?"

"You managed it between you anyhow," Arnold replied accusingly.

Pelling shook his head. "No, Inspector, that we most certainly did not. When Geoffrey sets out to commit a crime he takes no one into his confidence. Not even his sister; and she contrives to find out most of his business."

"How do you know that?" Arnold demanded.

"From my own experience," Pelling replied quietly. "Honestly, Inspector, do you really suppose when Geoffrey made these plans for murdering his nephew that he took me, of all people, into his confidence?"

"Never mind that. What do you mean when you say that you know from your own experience that when Geoffrey Maplewood commits a crime, he takes nobody into his confidence? What crime have you known him to commit?"

Pelling looked Arnold steadily in the eyes. "Perjury," he replied simply.

"Perjury? What do you mean?"

"The evidence that he gave at my trial was false from beginning to end."

Arnold made an impatient gesture. "I've heard that sort of thing before," he exclaimed contemptuously. "What's the good of trying to maintain your innocence after you've been convicted and served your sentence? And, besides, surely it's hardly playing the game to accuse Geoffrey Maplewood of perjury when he bought you out handsomely. You didn't say anything about it when we were talking about him the other day."

"Because I guessed then, as I might have guessed now, that you wouldn't believe me."

"How can I believe you in the light of the verdict? You're not suggesting that the judge and the jury were biased, are you?"

"Not for a moment. I had a perfectly fair trial, and no other verdict could have been reached on the evidence as it was presented. It was quite useless to deny that Geoffrey Maplewood's signature on the cheque had been written over a tracing. That was perfectly obvious to everybody, even the defence. I could only swear that I didn't do it, and I know well enough that my own counsel didn't believe me. It wasn't until afterwards, when I used to lie awake in prison and rack my brains until I thought I'd go mad, that I saw how the trick had been worked, and then, of course, it was too late."

There was something so convincing in Pelling's manner that Arnold was interested in spite of himself. "And how was it worked?" he asked indulgently. "You consider yourself a victim of persecution, I suppose?"

"I was the victim of a very ingenious plot, of which Geoffrey was the author," Pelling replied quietly.

"But what was the object of the plot? I can't see how Geoffrey Maplewood benefited by it in any way."

"The object of the plot was to send me to prison. And nobody can deny that it succeeded."

"But I don't understand," Arnold persisted. "You hadn't quarrelled in any way, from all accounts. What motive could Geoffrey Maplewood have had for sending you to prison?"

"Greed," Pelling replied swiftly. "Exactly the same motive, you observe, which led him to murder his nephew. As soon as he saw that the business was prospering, he wanted the whole of it for himself. You said just now that he bought me out handsomely. Well, people may be forgiven for supposing that to buy a convict out at rather less than a quarter of what his share was worth was a handsome act. And the joke is that he didn't buy me out with his own money. The solicitor let the cat out of the bag at the time. Geoffrey borrowed the money from his brother's estate. I wonder if he's paid it back yet?"

"You needn't have accepted what he offered you," Arnold objected.

Pelling laughed mirthlessly. "Oh, no, I needn't have accepted. But somehow I didn't feel like settling down again in Addleford with the glamour of prison shining round my head like an infernal halo. It was a choice of evils, and of the two I chose the lesser. And perhaps you can imagine that I didn't exactly want to go into partnership again with Geoffrey. You see, by that time I guessed how the trick had been played."

"I'm getting a bit tired of hearing about a trick having been played on you," said Arnold impatiently. "You admit yourself that Geoffrey Maplewood's signature on the cheque had been traced. If you didn't trace it, who did? Who had the custody of the cheque book, to begin with?"

"I can see that I shall have to tell you the whole story," Pelling replied wearily. "You won't believe it; but at least you will understand that my affection for Geoffrey is not so great that I should have obliged him by helping to murder his nephew.

"There's no need to go into much detail. But I must explain that Geoffrey and I were equally partners in the business. Roughly speaking, he looked after the office and I looked after the works. But he had as much right in the works as I had in the office. And, to answer your question, the cheque book was kept in a safe in his room, to which both of us had a key. The usual custom was for Geoffrey to make out cheques, sign them and pass them on to me for counter-signature. But the prosecution argued, quite rightly, that there was nothing to prevent me from getting hold of a blank cheque if I wanted to.

"What happened about the particular cheque in question was this: when I first saw Geoffrey one Monday morning he told me that he had hurt his hand at the farm on the previous day. As it happened, as he had contrived it, I hadn't been down with him that week-end. His hand was certainly bandaged, that's all I know.

"Later on that morning he asked me to come into his room. He told me that the business could now afford the sum which had been agreed upon between us for the invention. He showed me a cheque, which had nothing on it but his signature, and said that although he'd managed that he'd like me to fill in the rest, as he found writing very awkward. Of course, I didn't suspect anything. I filled in the cheque and appended my signature under his very eyes. There were no witnesses handy, for he chose the time when the office staff had gone to lunch."

"But, man alive, that's ridiculous!" Arnold exclaimed. "What about the carbon tracing found beneath the signature?"

"Like everybody else, you regard tracing as convincing evidence that the signature was forged," Pelling replied. "But a man can't forge his own signature, though there's nothing to prevent him tracing it out first if he wants to. Unfortunately for me, I didn't think of that until after the trial. I'd been such a fool as to trust Geoffrey implicitly, and it took me a long time to realize that he'd done the dirty on me."

Arnold shrugged his shoulders. The idea seemed preposterous. But it was perfectly obvious that Pelling believed in the truth of it and imagined that he had a genuine and bitter grievance against his former partner. As he had said himself, it was highly unlikely that he would have consented to assist him in the perpetration of a crime.

"Well, that's as it may be," said the Inspector after a prolonged pause. "Now, then, I'd like to see that bicycle of yours."

Pelling took him to a locked shed, which he opened. Within was a man's bicycle by no means new and fitted with a pair of well-worn Clincher tires, differing entirely in pattern from the wheel tracks in Queen's Wood.

Before Arnold left Orpington he asked the police there to make enquiries as to whether Pelling had been seen about between Saturday afternoon and Sunday noon. This done, he drove back to Addleford, arriving at the police station just as Garland was going out to lunch.

"Hallo! Back again?" said the Superintendent cheerfully. "Hope you've had a pleasant morning. We've been busy this end making exhaustive inquiries, both at Riverbank and the mill, and the result is that it's as certain as anything can be that Geoffrey Maplewood can't have communicated with Pelling in any way either on Friday or Saturday. Come along and have some lunch. You can tell me your adventures afterwards."

In the office, after a satisfactory meal, Arnold described his interview with Pelling. "He's a queer chap," he said, "and I'll admit that I can't quite make him out. But he swears that he didn't act as Geoffrey's accomplice, and I'm prepared to believe him."

"On his bare word alone?" Garland asked.

"No, for several other reasons. To begin with, he speaks as though it were a matter of course that Geoffrey Maplewood killed his nephew. Now, if you and I had committed a joint murder, and I fell under suspicion, I shouldn't insist on your guilt. I should be too afraid that if you were taxed with the job you would give the whole show away and so land me in the soup. That's reasonable, isn't it?"

The Superintendent nodded and Arnold continued: "The next thing is that Pelling made no attempt to put up an alibi. The guilty man invariably tries to make out that he was somewhere else when the crime was committed. But Pelling said, as casually as you please, that he couldn't produce any evidence to show where he was at the time. And this didn't seem to worry him in the least. I got the impression that he didn't regard my suspicions any too seriously.

"Then comes the strongest reason of the lot. It seems that Pelling is very far from being grateful to Geoffrey Maplewood. He told me an extraordinary yarn about that forgery business which I needn't repeat at length. The gist of it was that his partner had traced his own signature on the cheque in order to get Pelling into trouble. Having succeeded, he had him at his mercy, and bought him out for next to nothing. Whether or not this is true, Pelling is convinced of it and hasn't therefore any particularly friendly feeling towards his former partner. Far from helping him to commit a crime, I fancy he would have denounced him to you if he had suggested such a thing."

"Which he didn't," Garland replied. "As I told you before lunch, I'm quite satisfied that there was no opportunity for any communication between the two. So Pelling's dropped out of the picture?"

"I don't see how we can keep him in it. Mind you, it was only a suggestion of mine that he might have been the driver of the van. And now, I suppose, we've got to start all over again looking for the elusive George."

"Well, I had an idea about him, but it wasn't any more fruitful than yours," said the Superintendent. "It struck me that if Geoffrey Maplewood wanted a man to drive a van, a likely person for him to pick on would be his own chauffeur. So I had Saxby's movements traced. You remember that on Saturday he drove Geoffrey Maplewood and his nephew to Tenteridge and was then sent back here?"

"Yes, I remember that. He's supposed to have left Tenteridge some time after half-past three."

"Well, he was having his tea at home about five. He and his wife's family live in the lodge you may have noticed when you went to Riverbank. And at ten minutes to six he drove Miss Maplewood to the Institute and waited for her there till seven or thereabouts. After he got home he took his wife to the pictures. He slept at the lodge and at half-past eight on Sunday morning he was having his breakfast. So we can't make him fit the bill."

"What about one of the chaps who work at the mill?"

The Superintendent shook his head. "They've all been questioned—discreetly, of course. And they can all account satisfactorily for their movements, either on Saturday afternoon or Sunday morning. And your George must have been missing from his usual haunts from six o'clock on Saturday till somewhere about noon on Sunday."

"None of their alibis are suspicious, I suppose? You know what I mean, of course. I always begin to feel a bit doubtful when anyone comes out with an alibi too promptly. For instance, I say to Bill Smith, 'Where were you at twenty past six on Tuesday week?' If he immediately answers, 'I was walking up High Street on my way to the Pig and Whistle,' I am inclined to wonder how it is that he remembers so clearly what he was doing at that particular time and place. Most people's memories don't record times unless there is some particular reason for it.

"On the other hand, if Bill Smith scratches his head and looks thoughtful, I think I'm going to hear the truth. 'Last Tuesday week, you said? Let me see, now. That was the day the missus fell downstairs and broke her leg. What did I do that evening? I know: I went to the Pig and Whistle. I can't say rightly what time I got there, but it must have been before seven, for Jack Barnes came in then and we played a game of darts. And now I come to think of it, I'd nearly finished my pint before he'd turned up. It looks as if I must have got to the pub by half-past six. If you want to know where I was at twenty past, I should say I was walking up High Street on my way there.' That's the kind of statement that sounds more convincing to me."

Garland laughed. "And to me, top. But I can assure you that all the alibis of the millhands sound quite convincing. And you must remember that in a comparatively small town like this everyone knows everybody else. It is usually quite easy to confirm any individual's statement of his whereabouts."

"You're lucky," said Arnold. "As a rule, alibis are only convincing when they don't exist. And they are sometimes impossible to prove or disprove. Take the case of Bill Smith, for instance, with his prompt statement as to his whereabouts at twenty past six last Tuesday week. I go on to ask him, 'When did you get to the Pig and Whistle?' He replies, 'Just as the clock in the bar showed the half-hour.'

"Now all this sounds a little too pat to me. So I go to the Pig and Whistle and interview the landlord. Yes, he knows Bill Smith. Yes, he's one of his customers. Comes in now and again for a drink, just when it suits him. Yes, he's pretty sure he was in the bar one day last week. And that's as far as I'm likely to get with any certainty. I'm supposing the landlord to be absolutely honest and truthful, by the way. I may, after careful questioning, bring back to his memory that it was last Tuesday evening that Bill called at his house. But it is quite impossible for him to tell me what time he came in or when he left."

"In this case, fortunately, things are a bit simpler," the Superintendent remarked. "We know that George's actions extended over a period of eighteen hours at least. And I'm perfectly satisfied that none of the millhands were missing for all that time."

Arnold frowned. "And yet we know that George isn't really a figment of my imagination. He existed all right. Half a dozen people saw him, and three of these spoke to him. All their descriptions agree as well as you could expect. It's practically certain that he had something to do with Basil Maplewood's death. It is still more certain that he had no possible motive for murdering him. Even if the murdering of strangers was his hobby, he couldn't have brought off this particular one without the connivance of someone inside the house. And that someone must have been Geoffrey Maplewood.

"Now this connivance with Geoffrey can't have been accidental. He didn't just call at the door and say, 'Any nice murders you'd like done today, sir?' And Geoffrey didn't reply, 'Yes, there's my nephew I'd like to get rid of.' No, Geoffrey must have got in touch with him on Friday or Saturday, that's quite certain."

The Superintendent shrugged his shoulders. "Sorry I can't help you," he replied. "As I've already told you, I've made the most careful inquiries. The only people with whom Geoffrey Maplewood had any connection on Friday or Saturday were either personal friends or business acquaintances."

Arnold sighed wearily. "It would be nice, wouldn't it, if just for once something happened in this case that wasn't absolutely impossible," he said.

## CHAPTER THIRTEEN

THAT NIGHT Arnold found it impossible to get to sleep. His mind refused to be turned away from the puzzle which had brought him to Addleford. And, try as he could, it insisted on returning again to some insignificant detail.

The utterly unimportant things, like Geoffrey Maplewood's meanness about trifles. His former partner had attributed the murder of his nephew to greed. Well, that in a sense was understandable. Where thousands of pounds were involved, the covetous man might conceivably resort to extreme measures. But petty meanness was quite a different matter.

Think of the alterations to the master's house as a case in point. But the fact that Geoffrey Maplewood had bought Forstal Farm merely as a hobby showed that he had plenty of money to spare. Yet at the very house which he intended for his own occupation he spoilt the ship for a ha'porth of tar. Instead of employing an architect to supervise the work which had to be carried out, he left it to the local builder for the sake of saving a few pounds at most.

Arnold had examined the bathroom so thoroughly that he remembered every detail. The crookedness of the tiles on the walls; the rubber floor-cloth that fitted the room so badly; and those taps, just fitted to the ends of the water pipes a few inches above the bath. How much more would it have cost to have proper taps fitted to the bath itself? Not more than a few shillings at most.

There could be no doubt that Geoffrey was mean, very mean. And, when you came to think of it, this made the employment of an accomplice seem rather queer. The mysterious George must have demanded some reward for his participation in the crime. And directly or indirectly that reward must have been financial. Geoffrey would have to dip his hand pretty deeply into his pocket. And what assurance had he against subsequent blackmail?

Arnold's wakeful mind drifted from Geoffrey Maplewood's meanness to the utterly incomprehensible proceedings of George. That rope he had been seen to coil up just before he drove away from the house on Sunday morning. The rope itself was accounted for by this time. It was the cord described by both Burlap and

Swanley, with which George had tied the suitcase onto his bicycle. But why should he have been coiling it up when Bill Owens saw him? Because he had just used it for some purpose.

But what purpose, in heaven's name? Had he thrown the end of it like a lasso through the bathroom window? It would have been a very difficult feat; but it might have been just possible. And what would the feat have accomplished? Basil Maplewood most certainly had not been strangled.

Confound Hallam and his brother pathologists! They are ready enough to say how Basil was not killed. To every reasonable theory of the cause of his death they raised some technical objection. But they were jolly careful not to commit themselves to any theory of their own. They babbled about electricity and high tension transmission lines and the post-mortem effects of electrocution. What was the good of that when there was no source of electricity anywhere near the house?

Back again to George and his rope. The rope had been used to secure the suitcase to his bicycle. It was pretty certain that George had visited the house during the night riding on his machine. Had he left the suitcase and the rope there on that occasion? When Owens saw him, had he just picked them up again?

This at all events was a possible theory, but it had its limitations. Arnold was quite satisfied that there had been no communication between George and any inmate of the house on Sunday morning. It was not possible that George could have entered the house or Geoffrey Maplewood could have left it without the knowledge of Mrs. Dukes or her daughter.

But it was possible that Geoffrey, having finished with the suitcase, had deposited it outside the house at some time during the night. Surely that was a more promising line of thought. George had, round about midnight, brought the suitcase to the house on his bicycle. He had left it and the rope there and gone back to Queen's Wood. Some time between then and the arrival of the Dukes in the morning, Geoffrey had put them outside the house, probably in the shrubbery. At half-past eight next morning George had called in the van to pick them up. He had just done so when Will Owens saw him.

Very neat. But this theory involved the old unanswerable question: if the contents of the suitcase could be brought to the house on a push-bike, why was a 15-cwt. van necessary to take them away again?

Because, when they were taken away, they were heavier than when they were brought. That at least was one answer. In other words, the purpose of the van had been to remove something weighty from the house.

But that supposition involved quite a lot of difficulties. What was the object, and how had it been conveyed to the house? It was nothing that had been there on the previous day, for the Dukes would have noticed its absence. Nor had Geoffrey brought anything heavy or bulky with him when he arrived at the house on Saturday afternoon.

The longer Arnold considered the van, the more utterly purposeless did it—and its driver, too, for that matter—appear. If George had wanted the van for any honest purpose, he would not have given a false name and address. There was no crime involved in purchasing a second-hand van. And then that particular name and address; given, no doubt, in case the van should be seen in the neighbourhood of Tenteridge. Yes, but when you came to think of it, it was a pretty risky thing to do.

Look at it this way: George must have known that sooner or later someone would make inquiries about the van found abandoned in Burlap's yard. The registration number would show that it had been bought from Mr. Swanley, who would reveal the name and address of the purchaser. These pointed directly to Forstal Farm, and so to Geoffrey Maplewood. Why had George thus deliberately left a clue which would lead to his collaborator?

On the other hand, was it after all remotely possible that George had no connection with the death of Basil? If he hadn't, then what on earth was the meaning of the adventure? Why had the van been stored for the night in Queen's Wood? Merely to give George an opportunity of making a new set of floorboards for it? And yet there was convincing evidence that the van had not left the wood between Saturday evening and about eight o'clock on Sunday morning.

It took Arnold a long time to formulate any sort of theory to account for George and the van, on the supposition that they had no connection with the crime. At last he hit upon one which seemed to be fairly plausible. According to this, George was no longer a murderer, but merely a potential burglar, and an amateur at that.

At some time he had visited the Tenteridge district and noted several promising cribs ripe for cracking. He also discovered the convenient clearing in Queen's Wood.

On this particular week-end, having nothing better to do, he had decided to essay his skill. He would want something in which to take away the swag; hence the van. He drove it into Queen's Wood, and during the night sallied forth on his bicycle to reconnoitre. After all, it was merely a guess that his destination had been the master's house. He might have visited any one of the large houses in the neighbourhood. But for some reason or other his plans had been foiled. That was obvious, since no burglaries in the district had been reported. On Sunday morning he had packed up in disgust, driven the van to Burlap's yard and abandoned it. The breakdown outside the house had presumably been accidental.

There was just this in favour of the theory: A murderer, especially a murderer of the type of Geoffrey Maplewood, would be most unlikely to confide his scheme to an accomplice. The risk of subsequent blackmail, or of being given away to the police, was far too great. Was it not more likely that Geoffrey, having decided to eliminate his nephew, should have carried out the job single-handed?

But how, in the name of the Sphinx, how? How had Geoffrey, outside the locked bathroom, produced a shock which killed his nephew inside? How was it that whatever had caused the shock had left no trace whatever behind it?

A vague memory disturbed Arnold's mind, something he had heard someone talking about—Merrion, probably. He was always talking fantastic nonsense which meant nothing. A fabulous creature, a single glance from which was enough to cause the death of a person instantly. The name came to him after a few minutes restless turning. The basilisk. That was it. The impossibilities of this case were already so abundant that a fabulous monster more or less hardly made any difference.

Well, then, supposing that Geoffrey was the owner of a tame basilisk or some creature of similar breed. He held this up to the bathroom window at the moment his nephew was stepping into the bath. It dutifully fixed its baleful eyes on the unfortunate young man, and he promptly fell dead upon the floor. But then, Geoffrey was most certainly inside the louse, not outside it at the moment. This automatically brought George into the picture once again. George, this time with a basilisk inside his van. The rope, of course, had been the lead with which it was kept under control.

Impatiently Arnold assured himself that all this was utter nonsense. He had never read *The Murders in the Rue Morgue*. If he had, he might have pursued further his inquiries into murder by

animal agency. As it was, his mind wandered off into a consideration of Geoffrey's habits. Unsociable sort of chap to spend every
week-end alone, or practically alone, like that. Only once in a blue
moon did he invite anyone else to share his country retreat. Pelling, in the days when they were still partners. He must have found
his company congenial. Or perhaps it was merely that he wanted
to talk business with him, secure from interruption. His sister, very
rarely. And his nephew, apparently, more rarely still.

Was this habit of seclusion natural to him, or was it merely the
reaction to the company of his loquacious sister? Or, again, was it
a habit deliberately acquired for some deliberate purpose? Had the
master's house from the first been bought and adapted to be the
scene of an ultimate murder?

The suggestion, although apparently far-fetched, was not without its attractions. It presupposed that for years Geoffrey had con-
templated getting rid of his nephew. But that was not so utterly
unlikely as it seemed at first sight. According to Pelling, who at
one time had known him pretty intimately, Geoffrey from his boy-
hood had been jealous of Hithering Estate falling to his brother
and his brother's son. Perhaps, all along, he had intended to create
an opportunity for murder and to take advantage of it.

So a fresh light was shed upon the crime. It had not been a sudden inspiration evoked by Basil Maplewood's letter on Friday
morning asking if he could come for the week-end. It had been
deliberately planned for years in advance, every detail considered
and every possibility of failure provided against. Perhaps the mysterious means, whatever they were, had been in readiness for a
long time waiting until Basil should of his own accord walk into
the trap.

Either the necessary machinery had been amazingly inconspicuous, or it possessed an entirely innocent appearance. Arnold
inclined to the latter view. There must be, at this very minute,
something in the house, probably in the bathroom, something
which had the power of causing death and yet looking as innocent
as, say, a cake of soap. The Inspector determined that in the morning he would revisit the house and once more examine every single thing it contained.

But still sleep refused to come to him. Pelling's extraordinary
statement returned to his memory and refused to be banished. The
man seemed normal enough when one talked to him. Clever sort
of chap who knew how to make the most of his scientific training.
First of all he invented that paper stuff, and now he was experi-

menting with wireless waves and things of that sort. One wouldn't
have thought that he would have been such an ass as to commit a
silly forgery which was bound to be brought home to him sooner
or later. But those scientific chaps often had queer twists in their
make-up.

Of course he insisted in maintaining his innocence. But, then, a
certain type of criminal always did that in the face of the most
convincing evidence. Even when they had been convicted and
served their time. Pelling, in that respect, was no exception to the
general rule.

And yet in some ways he was rather exceptional. The protest-
ing criminal spoilt his case by exaggeration. You could tell by his
volubility that he wasn't telling the truth, like the men who come
round selling linoleum. But Pelling hadn't been like that. He d
made a statement of facts and left them at that. The explanation
being probably that he had brooded so long over his story that he
had come to believe in himself.

And a most astonishing story it was; astonishing because there
was nothing about it inherently impossible. The average criminal
proclaiming his innocence invented the wildest fables, all of which
could proved to be false. But Pelling hadn't done anything of the
sort. Geoffrey Maplewood might have traced his own signature on
the cheque and subsequently placed the incriminating evidence on
his partner's desk. None of the facts contradicted this theory. But
even if the suggestion had been made at the trial it would have
carried very little weight. It would have been one man's word
against another's and the Court would naturally have believed the
man who had apparently nothing to gain by the crime. Was Geoffrey capable of playing such a thoroughly dirty trick? At the time
no one would have thought so. Beyond a certain reputation for
meanness, he had seemed a respectable enough citizen. But now—
well, his character was by no means so blameless. No doubt he
had murdered his nephew. No one else had either the opportunity
or the motive. He had decoyed him to the house in Tenteridge for
that purpose alone. And his motive, as Pelling had expressed it,
had been greed. And if greed could incite a man to murder, surely
it could far more easily incite him to play a dirty trick on his partner?

There was then the disturbing possibility that, after all, Pelling's version of the affair might be the true one. Disturbing because, if so, there had been a grave miscarriage of justice. It was
Geoffrey who should have been convicted, and not Pelling. But

however disturbing this might be, there was nothing to be done about it. Even if the case were to be re-tried, Pelling could not prove his contention, especially after all this time when the material evidence would no longer be available.

Whether or not Pelling had invented the yarn, the very fact that he had told it showed that his former friendship for Geoffrey Maplewood had turned into bitter hatred. One doesn't accuse a man of a trick like that if one still retains a vestige of friendly feeling for him. That being so, it was in the highest degree unlikely that Pelling would have helped Geoffrey to murder his nephew. And if Pelling's story happened to be true, it was absolutely certain that Geoffrey would never have ventured to approach him with such a project.

But had he approached anybody? Was he the sort of person who would have trusted anyone with such a dangerous secret? Far from being a babbler, he seemed to be a man who kept his thoughts and his contentions to himself. His habit of secluding himself at the week-ends seemed sufficient evidence of that. But, then, if he had planned out the murder single-handed, where did George and his van come in? Pelling had already been eliminated. Were George and his amazing escapade to be ruled out, too?

So Arnold's sleepless mind revolved in a monotonous circle, until at last it went off at a tangent. After all, there was as yet no definite evidence that Basil Maplewood had been murdered. What other alternatives were there?

From all accounts, Basil had been an ordinary normal, healthy young man with a strong sense of his responsibilities. He had succeeded to the Hithering Court Estates and had taken a proper interest in their management. He had approved of his sister's engagement and was prepared to give her a hand some present on her marriage. He had been on sufficiently good terms with his uncle to suggest himself for a week-end in his company.

What had passed between them on Saturday evening? That would probably never be known. It was no use asking Geoffrey who, as the sole survivor of the conversation, would be free to put his own construction upon it. But, whatever the two may have discussed, there was very little doubt that Basil had broached the subject of the repayment of the money.

This, in any event, must have been distasteful to his uncle. Geoffrey Maplewood was not the type of man to part readily with a sum of ten thousand pounds. He had been evasive, probably, or, at the most, had given a reluctant promise. In any case, it was unlikely that there had been an open quarrel. Basil would hardly have stayed under his uncle's roof if they had had a serious difference of opinion.

Besides, his behaviour next morning seemed to show that he had nothing very disturbing on his mind. He had been asleep when Mrs. Dukes brought his tea. He had whistled cheerfully on his way to his bath. He had turned on the bath water and proceeded to shave in the most matter-of-fact way possible. And then—

And then he had died, suddenly and inexplicably; died in a room to which no other person could possibly have gained access. Could his death have been natural, or could it have been due to suicide or accident?

Arnold knew that now and then apparently healthy persons fell down dead for no visible reason. But he also knew that in such cases post-mortem examination invariably revealed some latent defect in the mechanism. A young and healthy human heart did not just stop beating of its own accord. In the light of the medical evidence, Basil's death from natural causes might be ruled out.

Suicide, then? But this was unthinkable. Why should Basil have decided to take his own life, and chosen the moment of stepping into his bath to carry out his intention? Besides, how had he carried it out? The bathroom contained nothing whatever with which he could have administered a shock to himself. He could have cut his throat with his razor or choked himself with his shaving brush or drowned himself in his bath. But he hadn't done any of these things. He had—well, just died, and that was all there was about it.

Remained the possibility of an accident. But what sort of accident? Driven to desperation by his inability to come to any sane conclusion, Arnold began to wonder if the doctors were so infallible as they pretended. Basil had fallen to the floor with some violence; the bruises on the body showed that clearly enough. Dr. Prescott had been positive that the injuries due to the fall had not been sufficient to cause death. But might not the shock of the fall have been fatal? In this case the whole mystery could be very easily explained, Basil, in the act of getting into his bath, had slipped on the rubber floor-cloth and fallen heavily. The resulting shock had killed him. And neither Geoffrey nor anyone else had had anything to do with the matter.

A delightfully simple explanation and one which, Arnold reflected, might commend itself to the coroner's jury when the inquest was resumed. But whether it was in accordance with the facts was quite another matter. It seemed extremely unlikely that a simple fall to the ground would be fatal to a strong and healthy young man. Some far more violent cause of shock must clearly have been responsible.

In which case, whatever had produced the shock must have left some trace behind it. The most trifling thing, perhaps, but still capable of being spotted by a sufficiently observant eye. The obvious course was to go through the house, and particularly the bathroom once again with the microscope.

Unless, of course, Geoffrey had somehow, contrived to remove the visible clue. The Inspector once more pictured the scene as it had been described to him. Reuben Dukes in the presence of his wife and daughter and employer had burst open the bathroom door. The attention of all four had, very naturally, been concentrated upon the body. Had any unfamiliar but not too conspicuous an object been the room, it was quite possible that it would have escaped their attention.

Good enough so far. Reuben ordered his wife and daughter downstairs, where they remained until they left the house. They had no opportunity of inspecting the bathroom in the interval. Reuben actually entered the room, but his concern was wholly with the body. This he lifted and carried into the bedroom. Having done that, he went downstairs and joined his family in the kitchen to await with them the arrival of the doctor.

According to the time-table which Arnold had compiled, at least quarter of an hour had elapsed between the removal of the body from the bathroom and its examination by Dr. Prescott in the bedroom. During this period the only living person on the upper floor had been Geoffrey Maplewood.

He would, then, have had ample time to remove the supposed object which had hitherto escaped observation. Had he done so, how would he have disposed of it? He would surely not have risked leaving it in the house, which was certain to be thoroughly searched. The alternative was that he had taken it away with him, first to the farm and then to Addleford.

But Geoffrey, leaving as he did a supply of clothing and so forth at the house, did not bring a suitcase with him on the occasions of his week-end visits. Any object which he had taken from the house must, therefore, have been small and light enough to be carried on his person. But what object fulfilling these conditions would have been capable of producing a fatal shock?

Any form of explosive was out of the question, for obviously there had been no explosion. The doctors had said that the post-mortem appearances were not unlike those found in cases of elec-trocution. Had Geoffrey concealed some electrical gadget in the bathroom? That was not of itself impossible. But the Inspector, although no expert, had at least a knowledge of the elementary properties of electricity. Enough, at all events, to convince him that no gadget capable of being carried in his coat pocket could produce enough electricity to kill a healthy young man.

Obviously the only thing to do was to make a thorough and minute search of the house and to keep on at it until something definite had been found. Arnold felt inclined to reproach himself for having put this off for so long. But, after all, a fellow couldn't be everywhere at once. The inquiries he had already made had been necessary, if only, for the purpose of establishing motive; except, perhaps, the day wasted on George and his adventure.

Arnold made a last determined effort to get to sleep, and this time succeeded. He dreamt that he was being driven by Pelling through tortuous country lanes in George's van, pursued by an infuriated basilisk.

## CHAPTER FOURTEEN

THE NEXT MORNING Arnold got up early, feeling jaded and unrefreshed. After he had trifled with his breakfast, Lambert drove him to the house. Terry was in attendance with the key, and under the supervision of the Inspector a minute search was made.

It lasted the whole morning until Arnold, greatly disheartened, called a halt for lunch. Absolutely nothing that could throw any possible light upon the subject had been discovered, in spite of the fact that the whole place had been thoroughly ransacked. The contents of every cupboard, drawer and box had been examined. Every piece of furniture had been moved or turned upside down. The carpets had been rolled up and boards removed from the floors for inspection of the spaces beneath them. With great exertion, Arnold had insinuated himself into the roof, where he found nothing but the cold water cistern.

He took his two subordinates to the Maypole at Tenteridge, where he ordered supplies of cheese and beer.

"There's nothing there," he said despondently, as he drove his fork into the pickled onion which Mr. Vincent had thrown in to give a zest to the meal. "If there was, we should have found it. We shouldn't have overlooked a black pin stuck in the soot in the chimney flue. What do you chaps think?"

Terry's mouth was at that moment too full for reply, but Lambert answered for the pair of them: "I don't think there's anywhere we didn't look, sir."

"I'm pretty certain there isn't," said Arnold. "What Mrs. Dukes and your girl friend will say when they see the place, I simply daren't contemplate. We've pretty well pulled it to pieces between us. This afternoon we'll have a look round outside in the flowerbeds and particularly in that shrubbery in front, just in case anything has been thrown out of any of the windows. Nobody's had a chance of getting into the garden, have they, Terry?"

"No, sir," Terry replied. "Either me or one of the other men has been on duty there since last Sunday."

"That's good. Our trouble is that we don't know in the least what we are looking for. The doctors say that the poor young fellow died of shock. And if either of you can think of anything that can have caused that shock I'll have a putty medal struck for you."

Lambert shook his head. "Shock's a queer thing, sir," he replied. "I had an aunt who saw an old toff knocked down by a motor bus. Standing close beside him, she was, when it happened. And she never properly got over it. She died within a twelvemonth, and we all said that it was the shock that had done it."

"I dare say you were right," the Inspector agreed cordially enough. "But Basil Maplewood wasn't looking out of the window when he died, and there weren't any motor buses running by the house at that time on Sunday morning. Can't you think of something else?"

Lambert shook his head and Terry tried his hand at the problem. "He might have heard something which upset him, sir."

"Heard what?" the Inspector asked.

"Well, I couldn't say for certain, sir. But I've heard of people falling down dead when someone told them a bit of bad news."

"Not healthy young men like this poor chap. Besides, what bad news could he have heard when he was getting into his bath? You, neither of you have earned the medal yet, I'm afraid. We'll just go back to the house when we've finished lunch and start again."

Terry took an envelope from his pocket and handed it to the Inspector. "You'll like to see that, sir. The postman delivered it at Forstal Farm this morning and Reuben Dukes gave it to me when he saw me."

The envelope was addressed to George Dukes, Forstal Farm, Tenteridge. It contained a request from the County Council for the production of the licence book referring to a Morris van, DD7241, purchased from Mr. Swanley, Woodcock Green. The book was required for registration of change of ownership, and a certificate of insurance must be enclosed.

"That confirms Mr. Swanley's statement," Arnold remarked. "It doesn't carry us any further beyond that. George isn't in the least likely to call at the farm for his letters. Now, then, if you chaps have had enough, we'll be getting back."

As they reached the house, Arnold remembered a remark made by Pelling when he had first interviewed him. The drains, and particularly the cesspit. It was a suggestion that might be worth following up. The Inspector led the way to the backyard outside the kitchen door, where he found an iron cover let into the concrete.

Under his direction, Lambert and Terry lifted this cover, revealing the interior of the cesspit, half full and distinctly malodorous.

"All right, put it back again," said Arnold hastily. "Are these things ever emptied—and if so, how?"

"The Council send a tank lorry round about once a month, sir," Terry replied. "That is, if you care to pay them for it. But nearly all the farmers round about do the work themselves. I know that Reuben Dukes sends round a couple of men with a barrel cart to empty this one, for I've seen them at it."

"Then we'll get him to pump it out straight away. We can't do anything with it until it's empty. All right, you carry on with the flower-beds. I'll tackle the shrubbery myself."

As Arnold set to work on his self-appointed task he was still thinking about the drains. The cesspit, of course, was only one end of the system. There were the pipes leading to it. He found four connections: one from the lavatory outside the back door, a second from a sink in the scullery, a third from the lavatory on the upper floor and a fourth from the bath and wash-basin.

As with the rest of the plumbing about the house, these connections were roughly constructed, but sound enough. The waste from the bath and the wash-basin, for instance, discharged through a metal pipe which ran down outside the house and emptied a few inches above a stone-ware gully. From the gully the water ran through an ordinary drain-pipe to an inspection chamber and thence into the cesspit.

The inspection chamber, almost hidden by the shrubbery, had a cover which Arnold with some difficulty managed to remove. The cavity beneath was clean, well flushed and absolutely empty.

Arnold replaced the cover and stood for a few moments in silent meditation. How could any object have been disposed of by way of the drainage system? Clearly by lifting the cover of either the cesspit or the inspection chamber, and dropping it in. But no one could have done this unobserved on Sunday morning between the time of Basil's death and the time when the occupants of the house left it.

But there was another method which might have been employed; provided that the object had been small enough. The gully receiving the waste from the bath and the wash-basin was almost directly underneath the bathroom window. There would be no difficulty in dropping an object from that window into the gully. A subsequent flush of water would carry it through the inspection chamber into the cesspit. How did that suggestion agree with the facts? During the period in which Geoffrey Maplewood had been left alone on the upper floor he could have entered the bathroom, where presumably the object already was. He could have picked it up and dropped it through the window into the gully. Then he could have turned on the tap from the washbasin—not that from the bath, for that was later found half full of water—with the plug out. The resulting flow of water would have taken the object into the cesspit.

If, then, the cesspit were to be emptied, the object might be found. But there was a snag here, as the Inspector realized. It didn't necessarily follow that the object was made of metal. It might have been made of some substance which by now had dissolved or become so corroded as to be unrecognizable. Still, that chance must be taken. The cesspit should be emptied at once and Reuben Dukes must be told to get on with the job.

Meanwhile, there was just a faint chance that the object had got lodged in the gully itself. Arnold, with a grimace of distaste, knelt down beside it. He rolled up his sleeve preparatory to putting his hand down the outlet. And then he noticed for the first time a slight but unmistakable scratch on the metal pipe just above it.

The only remarkable thing about this scratch was that it was fairly recent. Here and there where the paint had been scratched away the metal beneath showed bright. It was a trifling scratch, no wider than as though it had been made with the point of a knife. And as far as Arnold could ascertain, it ran horizontally the whole way round the pipe, two or three inches above the lower end.

It was impossible to guess what had caused this scratch, but it seemed pretty certain that it was not accidental. Nothing falling from the bathroom window could have made a scratch all the way around the pipe. It must have been made deliberately and by human agency. It bore evidence of having been made recently. It could not have been made since Sunday morning, for from that time a continuous watch had been kept upon the house. Therefore it must have been made shortly before Basil Maplewood's death.

After staring at it for some time, Arnold shook his head, feeling that the riddle was beyond him. He renewed his search for some more tangible object. Plunging his hand into the gully outlet, he groped about with his fingers. At the first attempt he retrieved half a dozen leaves which had obviously blown in from the shrubbery. At the second attempt something pricked his fingers, and after further groping he withdrew a short piece of fine wire. He continued his efforts until he could feel something else in the gully, by which time he had recovered three more pieces of wire.

All these pieces were similar in appearance, though not in length, which varied from two to six inches. The wires were no thicker than horse hair and of some tough, springy metal. Where had they come from, and how had they found their way into the gully? Here was another riddle to add to that of the scratch on the pipe. Or were there not two riddles, but only one? Had the pieces of wire caused the scratch? By the look of things, they were quite capable of having done so.

Having at last found something, though the significance of this discovery was still obscure, Arnold resumed his search. He examined the pipe, the wall of the house, the outside of the bathroom window, without further success. And then he turned his attention to the shrubbery which occupied nearly all the space between the house and the low wall bordering the road.

This shrubbery, which was evidently intended as a screen rather than an ornament, consisted of evergreen shrubs amongst which common privet predominated. The lower stems of the shrubs were bare and Arnold found it possible to crawl about among them on his hands and knees. But he found nothing to reward his perseverance. The ground was covered with dead and withered leaves, similar to those he had fished out of the gully. Lying on these, he happened to notice half a dozen fragments of fresh leaves which looked as though they had been torn from the shrubs. The work of some bird or insect, Arnold thought. But it was rather curious that these fragments of leaves should lie in a straight line running from the gully to the boundary wall.

Arnold extricated himself, dusted his clothes and then joined his two subordinates, who were still zealously searching the lawns and flower-beds on the farther side of the house. They had found nothing more stimulating than two very rusty trouser buttons. Arnold triumphantly produced his pieces of wire.

"What do you make of these?" he asked. "I found them in the gully beneath the bathroom window."

The two policemen surveyed the fragments respectfully. It was Terry who spoke first. "In the gully, sir? Looks like bits of a wire brush that had been used some time to clean out the drains."

But Lambert shook his head. "Not stout enough for that by a long way," he said sapiently. "It's more like the wire they use in flower shops to stiffen up bouquets. Or else—do you mind if I take up one of those bits, sir?"

"Not in the least," Arnold replied. "But I warn you that you won't find any fingermarks on them, or that if you do they'll be mine."

Lambert took a piece of the wire between his fingers, rubbed it clean with his handkerchief and bent it backwards and forwards tentatively.

"Excuse me a minute, sir," he said as he handed it back. He vanished, to return in a couple of minutes with a black, snake-like object which he dangled proudly before the Inspector's eyes.

"What have you got there?" Arnold demanded.

"A spare lead, sir. I knew I had one in the tool box of the car, and I thought you might like to see it."

"Why the devil should I want to see it?" Arnold demanded.

"Because it's made up of wires very like those which you've found, sir," Lambert replied. He produced a knife from his pocket and cut away a couple of inches of the heavy rubber insulation, thus disclosing a thin metal core, made up of several strands of fine wire twisted together. He unravelled one of these strands, cut off a length of it, and handed it to the Inspector. "I don't think you'll find there's much difference, sir," he said.

Arnold compared Lambert's sample with the fragments he had found in the gully. "There isn't," he replied. "What's that lead of yours used for?"

"It takes the current from the distributor to the sparking plugs, sir."

"The devil it does!" Arnold exclaimed thoughtfully. "It would carry any sort of current anywhere, I suppose?"

"It would if it was long enough and the current wasn't too heavy, sir."

"All right," said Arnold sharply. "It's time we packed up. It's getting too dark to see very much more out of here. You and I'll get back to Addleford, Lambert. You, Terry, had better stop here until you're relieved. I don't want anything about the place disturbed."

The Inspector sat wrapped in thought during the drive back to Addleford. He arrived at the police station, where Garland greeted him with his habitual cheerfulness. "Well, found anything?" the Superintendent asked.

"Yes, but I don't quite know what to make of it," Arnold replied. "Do you happen to know much about electricity.

"Just about enough to be able to change a fuse when one blows. Why?"

"Because I'm beginning to believe that Basil Maplewood may have been electrocuted after all, though I can't for the life of me see how. And it will take a bit of an expert to answer the questions I want to ask."

"Well, there won't be much difficulty in finding one, even in Addleford. I happen to know Welch, the manager of the local electricity works, fairly well, and I'm sure he'll willingly come round here if I ask him."

Arnold eagerly fell in with this suggestion, and in less than half an hour Mr. Welch was sitting in the Superintendent's office and being introduced to Arnold.

The Inspector first produced his fragment of wire. "Can you tell me what these are, Mr. Welch?" he asked.

Welch picked them up and handled them as Lambert had done. "They look to me like bits broken off the end of a high tension lead," he replied. "You know what I mean, I expect: the black rubber insulated wire used on cars, for instance."

"Yes, I know the stuff. How far could you carry current with a lead like that?"

"Practically any distance, I should think. But, of course, there would be a drop in voltage proportional to the length of the lead."

"Could you carry current from a fifty volt lighting plant to a point a quarter of a mile away?"

"Well, I suppose you could. But you wouldn't have much of a voltage at the far end of the circuit."

"Enough to kill anybody?"

"Good heavens, no! I doubt if you would feel it unless you put your tongue to the wires."

This disposed of one of the Inspector's queries. He had imagined current having been brought from the lighting plant at Forstal Farm to the house. The only other source of electricity in the neighbourhood was the grid system, which ended three-quarters of a mile from the house, and three-quarters of a mile of this lead was rather a tall order.

However, he put the suggestion to Welch, who shook his head doubtfully. "Only single-phase wires run through Tenteridge," he said. "That means that you can't get more than 280 volts at the most. Even supposing that you managed to get anything like that at the end of your lead, it's a thousand to one against your being able to kill anybody with it. I know there have been cases of death from the grid voltage—the voltage when stepped down for domestic use, I mean. But these cases are very rare, and it has nearly always been found that the victim had something pretty serious the matter with him before he got the shock."

"It's a fact, isn't it, that a man's more likely to get a shock when he's in his bath than when he's out of it?"

Welch smiled. "Well, that's one way of putting it. The reason is that wet skin is a better conductor than dry. We always recommend that special care should be taken with electric fittings in a bathroom."

"Then there's just a chance that if a man in the act of getting into his bath touched a lead carrying the grid voltage that it would kill him?"

"A very remote one," Welsh replied. "He'd probably get a shock which would make him more careful the next time. Of course I know what you're referring to all this time. Everybody's talking about the sudden death of Mr. Geoffrey Maplewood's nephew. But I'm bound to say that I don't see how he can have been electrocuted. He was in the act of getting into his bath when he died, so I've heard. You appear to have found traces of a high tension lead. But can you suggest how that lead was brought into the bathroom?"

"No, I can't," Arnold replied. "That's just what I'm up against. I'll tell you now exactly what I did find this afternoon: these bits of wire in the gully beneath the bathroom window; and on the metal pipe leading from the bath down to the gully I found a scratch, just as if the wire had been tied round it."

Welch laughed. "I'm afraid your discovery doesn't mean much, Inspector," he said. "If the lead was indeed taken into the bathroom, I don't see how—unless—by jove! that's an amazing possibility."

"What is?" Garland asked, astonished at the sudden display of interest in Welch's tone.

"I can't explain without exactly seeing the place," Welch replied excitedly. "But if the conditions happened to be favourable, it could be done. Naturally, I've got a professional interest in this. When can you let me have a look for myself?."

"Now, if you like," said the Superintendent. "Lambert can drive us over there in the car. It will be dark, but we can take torches with us."

Welch agreed to this suggestion with enthusiasm. In less than an hour the three of them had reached the house, to which they were admitted by Terry. Welch, who had been muttering to himself ever since they had left Addleford, ran upstairs a couple of steps at a time. Garland and Arnold found him eagerly investigating the bathroom by the light of a torch.

Arnold shrugged his shoulders. "We could do better than that," he said in a matter-of-fact tone. He struck a match and lighted the gas.

"That's better," said Garland. "You electrical chaps never think of any other means of illumination. Now, then, what about it?"

"It's marvellous!" Welch exclaimed. "Everything in the room might have been arranged for the very purpose."

"I dare say it was," Arnold remarked with a meaning glance in the Superintendent's direction. "But we're still waiting for you to explain."

"Explain!" replied Welch, gesticulating violently. "Can't you see for yourselves? Look at the rubber floor-covering, and the taps which don't touch the metal of the bath at all. What about the waste pipe? You said you thought the lead had been attached to it. Does it run all the way down to the ground?"

"No, it doesn't. It stops a few inches above the gully"

Welch fairly danced in his excitement. "Then don't you see that the bath is to all intents and purposes insulated? Just how was the man lying when he was found?"

"On his side on the floor with one leg hanging-over the edge of the bath," Arnold replied. "Just as though he was stepping into it when he was killed."

"But of course he was!" Welch exclaimed. "I can tell you exactly what happened, just as if I'd been here in the room at the time. He put one leg into the bath and found the water either too hot or too cold for his liking. So he reached to one or other of the taps. And the moment he touched either of them he was a dead man."

"I dare say it's plain enough to you," said Garland soothingly. "But you'll have to be a bit more explicit if you want us ignorant policemen to understand."

"Why, any elementary schoolboy could see how it was done," Welch replied scornfully. "Look here, to begin with, we've got to suppose some sort of electricity of fairly high tension. The ordinary domestic supply voltage wouldn't do. Nobody can tell how many volts exactly will kill any given individual with certainty. But I believe that when they electrocute folk in America they use a tension of 1,700 volts just to make sure.

"This source of electricity, whatever it was, was outside the house somewhere. I suppose I don't have to explain that an electric current only flows in a closed circuit. Very well. To one pole of the source a lead was taken to the waste pipe. The other pole was earthed by the simple process of leading a wire from a terminal of the apparatus to the ground. The circuit would not be complete, for the bath is insulated from earth. It stands on rubber, the taps don't touch it, and the waste pipe doesn't reach the ground. There would be some leakage where the waste pipe goes through the wall, but on a dry morning that wouldn't affect matters to any great extent.

"But see what happens when this chap gets into the bath. He puts one leg into the water. Still he's all right, for his other foot is on the rubber floorcloth, which insulates him from the earth. But then he puts his hand on the tap, and he's done for. A closed circuit is formed. The current runs from the lead to the waste pipe, the water in the bath, the man's leg, right through his body to his hand which is touching the tap. Finally, from this tap by way of the water pipe to earth. It's one of the neatest things I've come across in the whole of my experience."

"Yes, I dare say all that's simple enough," said Arnold doubtfully. "But there's just one little difficulty, you know. You talk about a source of electricity of high voltage. Where are you going to find that within a reasonable distance from here?"

The Superintendent stepped in before Welch could reply. "Isn't that where our friend George comes in? His van was standing outside at the time, you remember. And all motors have a magneto or other device for producing high tension current. It's what puts the spark into the sparking plug, I understand."

"Yes, and what's more, George left the engine of the van running," Arnold agreed.

But Welch shook his head in emphatic negation. "No, no, that's not it!" he exclaimed. "You would never get enough current from the electric equipment of a car to produce fatal results. It's a matter of internal resistance. I'm not going to explain. You'll just have to take my word for it. But a van, you say. What sort of a van?"

"Just an ordinary Morris commercial van of uncertain age and dilapidated appearance," Arnold replied. "You can see it for yourself, if you like. It's parked at Forstal Farm, just a quarter of a mile from here."

"And it was standing outside this house with the engine running when the man was killed?" Welch demanded excitedly. "Who is this fellow you call George and what was he doing with the van before he came here?"

"We don't know who he is," Arnold replied. "But apparently he spent part of the previous night fitting a new set of floorboards to the van, which suggests that he was an industrious sort of chap."

Welch snorted impatiently. "Floorboards? Bunkum!" he exclaimed. "You'd better let me have a look at that van and see what I can make of it."

They adjourned to the farm, where the van was standing in the cart shed. Reuben switched on the light for them and Arnold pointed out the floorboards.

"There you are," he said. "What he went to all that trouble for, I can't imagine. We found the old set of boards, and they weren't at all too bad."

"They weren't good enough for this purpose, evidently," Welch replied. "What did he cut those two slots in the centre board for?"

"So that he could put his fingers through and lift the boards out."

Welch raised his arms in despair at the Inspector's obtuseness. "Why did he go to the trouble of cutting two oblong slots when one plain hole would have been much easier to make and just as effective?"

"I wondered myself. He wanted something to do to fill in his time, I suppose."

"Not he. Those slots were cut for a very definite purpose. What do you imagine is underneath them?"

Arnold shrugged his shoulders. "I don't know." he replied. "Part of the works, I suppose."

"Part of the works! Haven't you ever examined the chassis of a car? I'll tell you what's underneath that floorboard and you can see for yourself if you don't believe me. The flywheel of the engine is directly underneath those slots. Now do you understand?"

"Not in the least," Arnold replied equably. "It's up to you to explain, Mr. Welch."

"I'll try. You've seen machinery driven by a belt, haven't you? Both the motors and the machinery to be driven are fitted with pulleys, and an endless belt runs round them. Now if you had a machine of some kind fitted with a pulley standing on this floorboard, you could run a belt round the flywheel of the van, through the slots, and round the pulley of your machine. In other words, you could drive the device from the engine of the van.

"And that, you may take it from me, is what your friend George did. He had some sort of electrical machine which would generate current at a high voltage. Or, for that matter, he may have gener-

ated at a low voltage and stepped in. The point isn't of any particular importance. And while he was standing outside the house with
the engine running, the poles of that machine were connected to
the waste pipe and to earth respectively. I'd like to know George.
He's a technician after my own heart."

"I'll see you're introduced as soon as I've got him in jug," Arnold replied. "But look here: a machine that would give all that
voltage would have to be a thundering great affair, wouldn't it?"

"Not necessarily," Welch replied. "Quite a small alternator, for
instance, hardly bigger than a model, would do the job if it were
properly designed for the purpose?"

"Could it be made small enough to carry in a suitcase?"

"I don't see why not. It would have to be designed to save all
possible size and weight, of course. Given time, I think I could
guarantee to get out the drawings for a machine which would be
capable of doing the job, and yet be quite portable. Although,
mind you, it wouldn't stand up to its work for any length of time."

"If it stood up long enough to kill Basil Maplewood that's all
George cared about," the Superintendent remarked. "I don't suppose he had any particular ambition to electrocute the whole family."

Welch waved this remark aside. "Let's have this floorboard out
and examine it more closely," he said.

"You'll find four screw holes in it set at the four corners of a
square," Arnold remarked.

"Yes, I can see them right enough. They're just behind the
slots, as you've probably noticed. I fancy that settles it. There were
four holes in the base plate of the machine, and George drove
screws through them and into the wood. That would hold the machine in position while it was being driven. Any more questions
you want to ask? If not, I should be glad to get back home. I'm
late for dinner as it is."

"I dare say we'll have plenty of questions to ask before we're
through with this business," Arnold replied. "I can't tell you how
grateful we are. You've shown us how the job was done, and
that's half the battle."

"What about the other half?" Welch asked.

"I think you can leave that to us," Arnold replied grimly.

## CHAPTER FIFTEEN

THAT EVENING Garland and Arnold met in the Superintendent's room. Neither had any doubt that the mystery of how the crime had been committed was solved. It remained now to bring it home to the criminal.

"George is our man, of course," said Arnold. "He actually worked the trick, although no doubt Geoffrey Maplewood put him up to it. We'd better begin with a reconstruction of the affair. We know now what the van was for. George didn't want it as a means of transport. He wanted the engine to drive his electrical machine."

"So that particular riddle is answered," Garland remarked.

"It is, thanks to your friend Welch. I don't flatter myself that I should ever have tumbled to it. Experts have their uses at times, as I've always said. George, equipped with his machine and a few other gadgets, knew exactly how to set about the job. No doubt Geoffrey Maplewood gave him all the necessary details, and perhaps the apparatus, too.

"At all events, George rolls up at Mr. Swanley's garage at Woodcock Green with his bicycle and suitcase. In the suitcase he had his electric machine, high tension lead and a few tools. He guessed that the floorboards in any old van that he might pick up wouldn't be stout enough for his purpose. No doubt, when he spotted the plank lying in the garage, he thought it would do. If there hadn't been one there, he would have got one somewhere else. He was bound to get hold of a bit of plank somewhere, because he couldn't very well have brought one with him on his bicycle.

"I shouldn't be surprised if he'd already had a look round at the likely garages on some previous occasion and seen that particular van for sale. He doesn't strike me as being the sort of chap who'd leave anything to chance. Or he may have been told of it. The point isn't of very great importance for the moment. He bought the van and drove it straight to Queen's Wood.

"I think now we can tell pretty well how he amused himself that night. He made the new floorboards, fixed the machine to them and connected up the belt. For reasons which we've already discussed, he probably didn't start on the job until after midnight.

And before he got to work he jumped on his bicycle and paid a visit to the house."

"For the purpose of settling final details with Geoffrey Maplewood?" Garland suggested.

"Not necessarily. The beauty of the scheme, as Welch explained it to us, was that it could be carried out entirely from outside the house. The doors and windows might have been bolted a thousand times, for all the difference it would have made. But there was one preliminary which George had to carry out. And for this it was essential that it should be dark, and that there should be no one about.

"When George left Queen's Wood on his bicycle, he took with him the high tension lead. He left his bicycle somewhere where it would not be seen by any passer-by and entered the garden by one of the two gates. From either of these it would be quite easy to get between the shrubbery and the house. Once there, he fixed the end of the lead, which he stripped of its insulation, to the bottom of the waste pipe. He didn't tie it. Just a turn or two and twisted the end over. The other end he led through the shrubbery to the boundary wall, leaving it on the ground inside. I expect he put a stone or something on top of the wall to show where the end of the lead was to be found. Then he left the premises, jumped on his bicycle again and rode back to Queen's Wood.

"Here, as I have already suggested, he rigged up his electrical machine. He had plenty of time to spare, for it wouldn't do to show up before it was absolutely necessary. Very likely he found time for a nap before he started out with the van. He seems to be quite a cool enough customer for that."

"Just one thing before you go any further," broke in the Superintendent. "How did George know what time Basil Maplewood would be having his bath?"

"That was arranged by Geoffrey, as we already know. Mrs. Dukes had orders to call both men at eight o'clock. Geoffrey sent a message to his nephew that he could have the first use of the bathroom. Basil's tea was presumably hot, and he would have to wait for it to cool. He would then go to the bathroom, where he would shave before getting into his bath. Geoffrey would be quite safe in telling George to be on the spot a little before half-past eight.

"George kept the appointment. As soon as he stopped outside the house, he fished for the end of the lead and connected it. He dropped another wire from the second terminal of his machine to the ground. We know that the bathroom window was slightly open. Probably Basil had opened it to let out the steam while the water was running into the bath. George heard the water running and waited. Then when the noise stopped he switched on the current. Basil may not have put his foot into the bath the moment he turned off the water. But he did a minute or two later. As soon as George heard the noise of the fall, he knew that the trick had worked, and switched off the current.

"All he had to do now was to recover the lead. Since he had merely wrapped the end of it round the waste pipe, that was a simple enough process. All he had to do was to pull on his end of the lead. And that's just what he was doing when Will Owens saw him. He was hauling in the lead and coiling it up as he went. And as the end came through the shrubbery it cut off a few leaves here and there. That accounts for both Owens' rope and for the bits of torn leaves that I found.

"The rest was quite simple. George drove away in the direction of Plaxted and pulled up at some secluded spot. Here he unscrewed his machine from the floorboard and disconnected the belt. We don't, of course, know what he did with these things. He is not likely to have left them by the roadside. I expect he put them back in the suitcase and subsequently took them home with him on the bicycle. I think we can flatter ourselves that our case against George is absolutely complete."

"Yes, that's all right," said the Superintendent thoughtfully. "But still, you know, the question remains: 'Where's George?' "

That question remained unanswered when the conference broke up well after midnight.

Arnold, after his previous restless night, slept soundly and woke next morning feeling refreshed and confident. All the most difficult features of the puzzle had been fitted together. The problem of how Basil Maplewood had been murdered in the locked bathroom had been solved. The conclusions of the doctors, ridiculous as they had seemed at first sight, had been justified after all. Basil had been electrocuted by some person unknown. Well, this person wouldn't remain unknown for very long. Arnold no longer had any doubts as to his next step. Hitherto his policy had been to bring the crime home to Geoffrey Maplewood through the medium of George. The thing to do now was to discover the identity of George through the medium of Geoffrey Maplewood.

From the first, there had never been the slightest doubt that Geoffrey was the instigator of the crime. The motive alone was sufficient demonstration of that. And now the facts made this even more clear, for no one but he could have forecast in advance the time at which his nephew would have his bath on that Sunday morning. And, for the matter of that, no one outside the household knew that Basil would be there at all.

Unless, perhaps, Mrs. Dukes might be held to have had the requisite fore-knowledge. She, better than anyone else, knew the rules of the house, which was that the occupants should be called at eight o'clock on Sunday morning. Geoffrey was noted for the regularity of his habits. It was most unlikely that he would alter his fixed rule on this particular occasion. Mrs. Dukes could have guessed the time of Basil's bath fairly accurately, but only if she knew that Geoffrey would invite his nephew to use the bathroom first. Could she have known in advance that he would do so? And what conceivable motive could Mrs. Dukes have had for procuring the murder of Basil?

No, she could be safely ruled out. Her employer was the only possible instigator of the crime, although it appeared now that he hadn't had the guts to carry it out himself. He employed an agent for the purpose, who had certainly dealt with the job discreetly and efficiently. Who could this agent have been?

The technique of the crime suggested someone with a scientific turn of mind and that in turn reflected upon Pelling. But, after all, it was no proof against him. Among Geoffrey's circle of acquaintances there must be many other people with a scientific turn of mind. Common sense alone established Pelling's innocence, for it was absolutely certain that under no conditions whatever would he have consented to murder Basil for his uncle's exclusive benefit. His expressed hatred of Geoffrey was far too deep for that.

Once more, and even more forcibly, this extraordinary aspect of the affair impressed itself upon the Inspector's mind. Geoffrey had employed an agent. Yet what possible inducement could have prevailed upon anybody to carry out such a calculated, cold-blooded crime? And again, would he voluntarily have put himself in the power of a man capable of such a deed? Yet there it was, there was no getting away from it. Geoffrey had by some extraordinary means found the man, for it was absolutely impossible that he and George could have been one and the same.

The longer Arnold pondered the matter, the more convinced he became that one of the pieces of the puzzle was missing; not a very large piece, perhaps, but of such importance that its insertion would alter the whole aspect of the picture. The key piece, in fact, upon which the whole pattern depended.

What was the link that bound George to Geoffrey Maplewood so firmly that he was ready to commit murder at his behest? All sorts of romantic possibilities suggested themselves. Geoffrey might have an illegitimate son, devoted to his father and his father's interests. But somehow that notion did not ring true. Romance and Geoffrey Maplewood had nothing whatever in common.

Yet the link must exist. It was quite impossible that George should be an amateur murderer, choosing his victims at random and, in this case, acting without any sort of understanding with Geoffrey. No stranger could have known the internal arrangements of the house, or the time at which the occupants had their bath. Nor, for that matter, would he have given the name of George Dukes and the address of Forstal Farm.

The link must exist. Common sense would allow of no alternatives. And yet, suppose, for one extravagant instant, that there was no collusion whatever between George and Geoffrey Maplewood? How, then, in the world did George come to know that Basil Maplewood was staying in the house that Sunday morning?

And then in a flash of inspiration the truth burst upon the Inspector's brain. George didn't know!

Burning with this revelation, Arnold lost no time in seeking out Garland in his office. "I've got it!" he exclaimed dramatically.

Garland's equanimity remained undisturbed by the Inspector's sudden entry. "Got what?" he inquired. "Nothing catching, I hope. You look a bit feverish, if you don't mind my saying so."

"I've got the solution to the puzzle," Arnold replied. "It's one of the most extraordinary cases I've ever heard of. Look here, it's a fact that Geoffrey Maplewood was in the habit of going down to the house at Tenteridge every week-end, isn't it?"

"I don't think there's the slightest doubt about that," the Superintendent replied.

"And going there by himself? Taking nobody with him, except perhaps once or twice a year?"

Garland nodded. "That seems to have been the case."

"You're pretty sure that Geoffrey didn't communicate with the man we call George after he knew that his nephew was coming for the week-end?"

"I'm practically certain of it. He didn't communicate with anybody we can't account for."

"Then don't you see that the odds are something like twenty to one that Geoffrey and no one else would be sleeping in the house that night? And that George had no means of knowing that, for once, Geoffrey had a visitor staying with him?"

The Superintendent scratched his nose reflectively. "I see that all right. But all the same, the fact remains that George did murder Basil Maplewood."

"Of course he did!" said Arnold with a heavy blow of his fist upon the table. "But it was an accidental murder. He bumped off the wrong man."

"Great Scott!" exclaimed Garland. "You mean that it was Geoffrey and not his nephew that he was after?"

"Of course it was! Just think what would have happened if Basil hadn't invited himself to stay with his uncle for the weekend. Geoffrey would have gone along to the house on Saturday and slept there that night. He would have been called at eight o'clock. Mrs. Dukes would have brought him his tea, and when he had drunk this he would have gone to the bathroom. George, waiting outside with his van, would hear the water running and switch on his current at the right moment; and the body found on the floor would have been Geoffrey Maplewood's."

"Wait a minute," said the Superintendent. "Let's get this straight, You mean that Geoffrey had nothing to do with his nephew's death?"

"I mean that, far from being the murderer, he was the intended victim. It's this motive business that's been queering our pitch all along. Everything pointed to Geoffrey having a motive for murdering his nephew. And it was just as clear that nobody else had the slightest motive for doing so. Now, we've got to get all that out of our minds and look round for someone who had a motive for murdering Geoffrey."

The Superintendent smiled, "I think I can guess who you've got in mind."

"I expect you can. But there are other things besides motive. We couldn't understand how George could have known the routine of the house and its internal arrangements. The only possible suggestion was that Geoffrey had told him. But if George had at some time stayed at the house, he could have found out all these details for himself. The time when Geoffrey liked to be called and the way the bathroom was fitted up, for instance."

"And from what you've told me about Pelling in his new role, he seems to be a bit of an electrician into the bargain," Garland remarked.

"Exactly. He's the very man to have fixed up the electrical machine that did the trick. That Pelling is fair and George is described as dark doesn't mean anything. It's easy enough with a little hair dye and a false moustache to fake up a disguise that strangers wouldn't notice.

"I told you what Pelling said about the forgery business. I'm inclined to believe now that his version of the affair is actually the truth. If it is, he had as rational a motive for murder as ever man had. Just think, a stretch in gaol and being shouldered out of his own business. You can't very well blame him for wanting to get his own back on his former partner.

"If my guess is right, we know now how he tried to do it. And as he drove away from the house that Sunday morning he must have chuckled at the success of his little scheme. It wasn't until I turned up at his place a couple of days later that he heard of his unfortunate mistake.

"Mind you, I don't think he was a bit surprised to see me that day. He must have known that when Geoffrey Maplewood was found dead the police were bound to interview his former partner sooner or later. He was prepared for that, I haven't a doubt. What he wasn't prepared for was the news that the dead man was not Geoffrey, but his nephew."

"It must be a bit of a shock to one that one has murdered the wrong man by mistake," the Superintendent remarked.

"It was a shock to Pelling all right. I'm sure of that. He looked utterly flabbergasted when I told him. It's not so much the poor chap's death that upset him, I imagine, although he did say more than once that nobody regretted it more than he did. Pelling had made up his mind to murder; and, after all, accidents will happen. It was the realization that all his time and trouble had been wasted and that he'd have to start all over again that shook him up.

"He played a pretty clever game with me, I'll admit. As soon as he saw that we suspected Geoffrey, the great idea came to him. If our suspicions could be made sufficiently strong, Geoffrey would eventually swing for the crime and Pelling would get his revenge after all without further trouble on his part.

"So, as artfully as he could, he bolstered up the theory of motive. I dare say that everything he told me about Geoffrey's resentment at not inheriting the estate was strictly true. But, all the

same, it was Pelling's job to weigh the balance as heavily as possible against Geoffrey. And at the same time he had to satisfy me
that he had not acted as Geoffrey's accomplice."

"Yes, his behaviour after the crime was pretty shrewd,"
Gailand agreed. "And, for that matter, the crime itself was remarkably well thought out. If you hadn't seen the scratch on the
waste pipe and found the bits of wire in the gully, we should never
have tumbled to how it was done."

"That's just what he counted on. He had to take the risk of the
van being seen and heard outside the house. But, properly handled,
the risk was so slight as to be negligible. What possible association
could there be between the van and the body of Geoffrey Maplewood found in the locked bathroom?

"You've got to remember that it was the suspicion of murdering Geoffrey Maplewood that Pelling had to avoid. If the crime
had come off according to plan, what would have happened? We
should have been up against the body found in a locked bathroom,
with no one but Mrs. Dukes and her daughter in the house. I don't
think we should have believed either of them guilty, even if we
could have formed any theory of how they had done the job. Respectable farm bailiffs or their families don't kill their employers
just for the fun of the thing; and in this case none of the Dukes
would have anything whatever to gain by Gregory's death. And
yet our attention would have been focused upon them when we
found the van and heard that it had been bought by a man who
gave his name as George Dukes.

"As I said just now, Pelling expected a visit from the police,
and I haven't a doubt that he'd got everything pat. He wouldn't
have said a word about the way in which Geoffrey had done him
over the forgery. He only brought that up when I accused him of
being his late partner's accomplice. It was the surest way of coun-
tering my accusation. His line would have been to be shocked and
horrified at the death of his benefactor, who had befriended him
after he had disgraced himself. And if he had taken that line, we
should never have guessed that he had any motive for the crime."

"I wonder what we should have guessed," the Superintendent
remarked thoughtfully.

"I don't know," Arnold replied. "But I feel pretty sure that Pelling would have got away with it."

Garland laughed. "It's a pretty queer business, whichever way
you look at it. A man devises a highly ingenious method of murder
and puts it into operation. Owing to circumstances which he could

not have foreseen, he kills the wrong man. I agree with you that if he had bumped off his intended victim he would never have been caught, but owing to his unfortunate mistake we've got him by the short hairs. You'll be taking a trip to Orpington, I expect? I'd like to come with you, if you don't mind."

A few minutes later they started out in the police car with Lambert driving and another constable in attendance. When they reached Orpington they called at the police station and made certain arrangements. As a result of these, a cordon of police unobtrusively surrounded Mr. Ernest's premises.

When the cordon was in place, Arnold and the Superintendent entered the shop. The Inspector, recognizing one of the girls he had spoken to on a previous visit, beckoned to her. "Tell Mr. Ernest that we should like to see him in his office," he said.

"Rightie-o," replied the girl, apparently unimpressed by the Inspector's manner. "I'll tell him."

She flounced forth, leaving the two policemen waiting impatiently in the shop.

"Where's that girl got to?" Arnold growled after a few moments. "The chap can't have bolted when he saw us coming, can he?"

"Not likely," Garland replied soothingly. "And, even if he had, he won't get far with all those men outside."

But it was fully five minutes before the girl reappeared. "Sorry to keep your lordships waiting," she said pertly. "But Mr. Ernest's not in his office. I went upstairs to look for him, but he wasn't there either. And then I thought of the laboratory and knocked on the door, and he was inside. He'll see you there if it's all the same to you. This way, please."

Arnold brushed her aside. "You needn't trouble to show us," he said curtly. "I've been here before."

Followed by the Superintendent, he strode through the shop towards the laboratory. The door was ajar, and when Arnold knocked upon it Pelling's voice bade them come in.

The interior of the laboratory was very much the same as Arnold had seen it on the occasion of his first visit. The benches lining the walls were crowded with instruments, familiar and unfamiliar. Pelling was at the farther end of the room, bending over some apparatus which emitted a high humming note.

He turned round as the two entered, without, however, advancing towards them.

"Good morning, Inspector," he said affably. "Becoming quite a regular visitor, aren't you? Who have you brought with you this time? Why, surely it isn't my old friend Superintendent Garland, whom I got to know so well at Addleford?"

"Yes, I am Superintendent Garland," was the reply; "and you are Ernest Pelling. Listen to me."

"Oh, I'm listening all right," said Pelling. "I'm quite sure that you've got something interesting to tell me. But I'd like you to know that you are interrupting me at rather an awkward moment. I've just started an experiment which I rather fancy will turn out to be the most important I've ever made. However, carry on with whatever you've got to say."

During this conversation, Arnold employed his mind in observing the details of the scene. The apparatus from which the high note proceeded was invisible, for it was screened by a piece of wood set up in front of it. On the floor before the bench lay a flat metal plate, and on this Pelling was standing. Another metal plate, considerably larger, lay farther out in the middle of the room, the two-plates being separated by a foot or eighteen inches.

"You will have to abandon your experiments," said the Superintendent shortly. "Ernest Pelling, I arrest you for the murder of Basil Maplewood. And I warn you that any statement that you may make may subsequently be used in evidence."

At this accusation, Pelling's nonchalant manner fell from him. "Arrest me!" he exclaimed. "Never! You've done that once before, and I'll take care that you don't do it again."

He turned to the bench behind him and picked up the first thing that came to his hand. It happened to be a length of glass rod, which he brandished threateningly.

"Come on, both of you," he challenged. "I'm a match for any two blasted cops, as you'll pretty soon find."

"Put that thing down and don't make a fool of yourself," Garland commanded sternly. "You might be a match for the two of us, but you wouldn't be for the dozen men we've got outside. Put it clown, I say."

As he spoke, both policemen moved forward, Garland leading, until his foot was on the larger of the iron plates. But Pelling, far from putting down the glass rod, continued to threaten them with it. "If you come any closer I'll smash your head in," he declared.

The Superintendent shrugged his shoulders. "You may just as well save yourself the trouble," he replied quietly.

He was just about to stretch out his hand to arrest the other's uplifted arm when, in a flash, Arnold realized the trap that had been set for both of them. With both arms he clasped the Superintendent round the waist and drew him bodily backwards till both his feet were off the metal plate.

Garland recovered himself and turned round to face the Inspector. "What the devil are you playing at?" he asked angrily.

But it was Pelling who replied with a burst of hysterical laughter. "So you've found out how it was done?" he said. "Well, you've got more intelligence than I should have suspected on my first acquaintance with you. But it wasn't Basil Maplewood I meant to kill. It was that swine Geoffrey, who deserves to die if ever a man did."

"A most regrettable mistake," said Arnold quietly. "Now that you've admitted the crime, you may just as well stop those monkey tricks of yours and come along quietly."

"Oh, I'll come quietly enough," Pelling replied. "But not under your custody, Inspector."

He took a step forward towards them, his right foot remaining on the smaller metal plate nearest the bench. As soon as his left foot touched the larger plate he seemed to leap into the air then fell with a crash upon the floor.

## CHAPTER SIXTEEN

I T WAS Arnold who spoke first. "No, don't touch him," he said as the Superintendent started forward. "He's as dead as Basil Maplewood. Now how do we switch off that infernal machine of his, I wonder?"

He made his way cautiously round the metal plates to the bench before which Pelling had been standing. Looking over the wooden screen, he saw a small machine, not unlike a dynamo in appearance, driven at high speed with a belt from an electric motor. He very soon found the switch which controlled the motor and switched it off. The high note fell rapidly down the scale, became a deep hum, and finally ceased.

"All safe now, I think," he said. "But just to make sure, we won't touch him until he's clear of those confounded plates. Catch hold of the collar of his coat and help me to pull. That's right. Now let's see if there's any life left in him."

For ten minutes or more they tried artificial respiration, but without any response from the inanimate body.

"Yes, he's dead all right," the Superintendent said at last as they desisted from their efforts. "But I confess I'm still in the dark. Why wouldn't you let me catch hold of him just now?"

"Because you'd have been in the dark for good and all if you'd touched him," Arnold replied. "Don't you see the idea? He's got one terminal of that infernal machine of his connected to each of these metal plates. You remember what your friend Welch told us? No current flows except through a closed circuit."

Garland glanced at the body. "A pretty good dose of current seems to have flowed through this circuit," he remarked.

"Yes, and I'll explain how and why. While Pelling was standing on the smaller plate he was all right. While you had a foot on the larger plate you were all right, too. Pelling's idea was to make a show of violence. He probably hoped to get us both with our feet on the larger plate; then, if we hadn't tumbled to his little game, we should have closed with him, and our numbers would have been up. As soon as we touched him the circuit would be complete and the three of us would have fallen in a heap on the floor. The fact is, my friend, that I saved your life just now, and you don't even seem decently grateful."

"I'm grateful enough now that I understand," Garland replied. "By jove, I don't believe I've ever been so near death as that."

"Let's hope you won't be till your time comes. Pelling didn't mean to be arrested, that's quite clear. He's had one experience of the dock, and he didn't want another. He preferred a quick and painless death, and I suppose he thought that he might just as well let us share it with him. But when he saw it wouldn't work, he stepped forward until he had one foot on each of the plates, and that did it."

Mr. Welch, summoned to the scene as an expert, confirmed Arnold's interpretation of events. He examined the apparatus on the bench and fell into ecstasies over it.

"It's really an exquisite bit of work," he said. "I said yesterday evening that a small alternator would produce the necessary current. And that's just what this is—a model alternator wound, by the look of it, to give between 1,000 and 2,000 volts. I haven't a doubt that Pelling made it himself, but it is by no means an amateur job. It's the work of a thoroughly skilled engineer."

"Do you think it's the same apparatus that he used to kill Basil Maplewood?" Arnold asked.

"I haven't a doubt of it," Welch replied. "It's no larger than was absolutely necessary to do the job, and its weight has been cut down in every possible way. I don't suppose it weighs more than ten or a dozen pounds at most. There wouldn't be the slightest difficulty about carrying it in a suitcase. And look here, you see those four holes in the base plates? Well, I don't mind betting you that they register exactly with the screw holes in the floorboards of the van."

Welch proceeded to trace the connections and found, as Arnold had guessed, that the terminals of the alternator were respectively connected to the two metal plates.

"That was a lucky hunch of yours, Inspector," he said. "If the two of you had gone for the chap there'd have been three bodies instead of one to be accounted for. What are you going to do with the alternator?"

"You'd better take charge of it," the Superintendent replied. "We shall want some technical particulars at the inquest."

"I'd like nothing better," exclaimed Welch enthusiastically. "I'll make a thorough examination of it and let you have my report. And on one condition I won't ask you any fee for that, either."

Garland smiled. "What's the condition, Welch?' he asked.

"That you allow me to keep this lovely little alternator as a souvenir," Welch replied.

That evening in the Superintendent's room a Addleford, he and Arnold sat discussing the various aspects of the case.

"It's all as clear as daylight now," said Garland. "But there is just one thing we shall never know. Was Pelling guilty or not guilty of forging his partner's signature to that cheque?"

Arnold shrugged his shoulders. "It's impossible to say," he replied. "It's no good asking Geoffrey Maplewood, of course. He'd merely stick like a leech to the story he told at the trial. Personally, although Pelling was the self-confessed murderer, I'm inclined to believe his version of the affair. At all events, I'm pretty well convinced that he believed it himself."

"If he did, his motive is fully established. The only thing that surprises me is that he didn't make his attempt on Geoffrey's life long before he did."

"I don't think that's very surprising," Arnold replied. "It wasn't the sort of crime that could be committed on the spur of the moment. We'll suppose, if you like, that Pelling came out of quod resolved to revenge himself upon Geoffrey. But he hadn't made up his mind how he was going to set about it. He probably thought of many different ways, and rejected them all until at last the bright idea came to him. And still he had his preparations to make. The alternator, for instance. Welch was certainly right when he said he'd made it himself. I'm no engineer, but I should imagine that to make a piece of machinery like that single-handed would take a very considerable time."

The Superintendent nodded. "I've no doubt it would," he said. "And there's another consideration which may have induced Pelling to bide his time. If Geoffrey had been killed too soon after his former partner's release from prison, we might have put two and two together. Pelling had to allow time for his former activities to be forgotten. He had to create a new personality: that of Mr. Ernest, the owner of the wireless business at Orpington. I don't suppose for a moment he imagined that the police would be unable to identify Mr. Ernest as Mr. Pelling. But if he waited long enough, there was at least a chance that Pelling's name would never come into the affair at all."

The coroner decided that an inquest on Pelling's body should be held before that on Basil Maplewood's was resumed. The former was a very brief affair, at which the Superintendent and Arnold were the principal witnesses. For once the jury made no reference to the state of mind of the deceased. With commendable promptitude they brought in a verdict of *felo de se*.

The resumed inquest on Basil Maplewood's body was naturally a more complicated affair. The police relied mainly upon the words spoken by Pelling immediately before his death and made no attempt to probe into his motive.

But the technique of the crime was adequately explored and supported by expert witnesses, Dr. Hallam and Mr. Welch among them. The latter replaced the alternator on the floorboards of the van and explained its mechanism to the jury. In his enthusiasm he would no doubt have repeated the experiment in its entirety could he have found a willing victim. The result, as Arnold had anticipated, was a verdict of Wilful Murder against Ernest Pelling, deceased.

But after the inquest Arnold and the Superintendent called upon Geoffrey Maplewood. In the course of the interview they hinted to him Pelling's version of the forgery, and asked him if he had any comment to make.

Geoffrey, though fearfully shaken by the knowledge that he had been the intended victim of the murder, indignantly denied that there was a grain of truth in Pelling's story. And since by this time there were no means of either proving or disproving Pelling's statement, they were compelled to leave it at that.

But either his narrow escape from death or his consciousness of guilt wrought at least a temporary change in Geoffrey Maplewood's character. The first evidence of this was his behaviour towards his niece. Phoebe, convinced by the evidence given at the inquest that he had not been responsible for her brother's death, made him a handsome and charming apology. Geoffrey, in turn, told her that he meant to adhere to his nephew's wishes, and to give her the ten thousand pounds which had been promised her on her marriage.

Pelling's estimate of his former partner's ambitions may have been correct after all. In any event, he announced that in future his life would be devoted to the maintenance of the Hithering Court Estate. Both the Addle Paper Mill and Forstal Farm were advertised for sale. Very much to everyone's astonishment, Geoffrey made a handsome cash payment to all his employees, not forgetting Reuben Dukes and his family.

A couple of months or so after the conclusion of the case, Arnold received a letter from Superintendent Garland.

"I know that you'll be glad to hear that the chief constable has considered your recommendation, and that Terry has been promoted to the rank of sergeant. He thoroughly deserves this step for the work he did in connection with the Maplewood affair, and I'm very glad to say that he's shaping very well in his new rank.

"There have been several changes locally since I last saw you. The paper mills have changed hands and are now, as the publicans say, under entirely new management. Forstal Farm is also sold, but Reuben Dukes continues in his old position as bailiff. Talking of Reuben and his family, you won't be altogether surprised to hear that Hetty Dukes and Lambert have fixed it up between them to get married before Christmas. The only one of your friends who remains with us is Miss Monica Maplewood, who now reigns in solitary state at Riverbank. She told me not long ago that although it tore her heartstrings to desert her brother, she felt that it was her sacred duty to remain in Addleford as Lady Patroness of the I.I.I.

"I saw Dr. Prescott the other day and told him that I would be writing to you shortly. He's still very much impressed by the way in which you found the essential clue. And he's immensely proud of the fact that at his very first examination of the body he found the true cause of death. I haven't a doubt that it has increased his reputation with his patients.

"Well, all the best, and if you're ever down this way again, mind you look in and see me. In any case, if we have any more mysterious murders in these parts I'll send for you at once."

But, in her own eyes, the heroine of the affair was Miss Monica Maplewood. She had listened to the evidence at the inquest without in the least comprehending it. However, in some hazy way, she had grasped that the murderer had made use of the waste pipe in the bathroom. And by some curious mental process she reasoned that this fact gave her the credit for having solved the mystery.

"The first time I saw him I told the man from Scotland Yard that it had something to do with the drains!" she exclaimed triumphantly.

THE END

# RAMBLE HOUSE's

## HARRY STEPHEN KEELER WEBWORK MYSTERIES

(RH) indicates the title is available ONLY in the RAMBLE HOUSE edition

The Ace of Spades Murder
The Affair of the Bottled Deuce (RH)
The Amazing Web
The Barking Clock
Behind That Mask
The Book with the Orange Leaves
The Bottle with the Green Wax Seal
The Box from Japan
The Case of the Canny Killer
The Case of the Crazy Corpse (RH)
The Case of the Flying Hands (RH)
The Case of the Ivory Arrow
The Case of the Jeweled Ragpicker
The Case of the Lavender Gripsack
The Case of the Mysterious Moll
The Case of the 16 Beans
The Case of the Transparent Nude (RH)
The Case of the Transposed Legs
The Case of the Two-Headed Idiot (RH)
The Case of the Two Strange Ladies
The Circus Stealers (RH)
Cleopatra's Tears
A Copy of Beowulf (RH)
The Crimson Cube (RH)
The Face of the Man From Saturn
Find the Clock
The Five Silver Buddhas
The 4th King
The Gallows Waits, My Lord! (RH)
The Green Jade Hand
Finger! Finger!
Hangman's Nights (RH)
I, Chameleon (RH)
I Killed Lincoln at 10:13! (RH)
The Iron Ring
The Man Who Changed His Skin (RH)
The Man with the Crimson Box
The Man with the Magic Eardrums
The Man with the Wooden Spectacles
The Marceau Case
The Matilda Hunter Murder
The Monocled Monster

The Murder of London Lew
The Murdered Mathematician
The Mysterious Card (RH)
The Mysterious Ivory Ball of Wong Shing Li (RH)
The Mystery of the Fiddling Cracksman
The Peacock Fan
The Photo of Lady X (RH)
The Portrait of Jirjohn Cobb
Report on Vanessa Hewstone (RH)
Riddle of the Travelling Skull
Riddle of the Wooden Parrakeet (RH)
The Scarlet Mummy (RH)
The Search for X-Y-Z
The Sharkskin Book
Sing Sing Nights
The Six From Nowhere (RH)
The Skull of the Waltzing Clown
The Spectacles of Mr. Cagliostro
Stand By—London Calling!
The Steeltown Strangler
The Stolen Gravestone (RH)
Strange Journey (RH)
The Strange Will
The Straw Hat Murders (RH)
The Street of 1000 Eyes (RH)
Thieves' Nights
Three Novellos (RH)
The Tiger Snake
The Trap (RH)
Vagabond Nights (Defrauded Yeggman)
Vagabond Nights 2 (10 Hours)
The Vanishing Gold Truck
The Voice of the Seven Sparrows
The Washington Square Enigma
When Thief Meets Thief
The White Circle (RH)
The Wonderful Scheme of Mr. Christopher Thorne
X. Jones—of Scotland Yard
Y. Cheung, Business Detective

## Keeler Related Works

**A To Izzard: A Harry Stephen Keeler Companion** by Fender Tucker — Articles and stories about Harry, by Harry, and in his style. Included is a compleat bibliography.

**Wild About Harry: Reviews of Keeler Novels** — Edited by Richard Polt & Fender Tucker — 22 reviews of works by Harry Stephen Keeler from *Keeler News*. A perfect introduction to the author.

**The Keeler Keyhole Collection:** Annotated newsletter rants from Harry Stephen Keeler, edited by Francis M. Nevins. Over 400 pages of incredibly personal Keeleriana.

**Fakealoo** — Pastiches of the style of Harry Stephen Keeler by selected demented members of the HSK Society. Updated every year with the new winner.

# RAMBLE HOUSE's OTHER LOONS

**The End of It All and Other Stories** — Ed Gorman's latest short story collection
**Four Dancing Tuatara Press Books** — *Beast or Man?* By Sean M'Guire; *The Whistling Ancestors* by Richard E. Goddard; *The Shadow on the House* and *Sorcerer's Chessmen* by Mark Hansom. With introductions by John Pelan
**The Dumpling** — Political murder from 1907 by Coulson Kernahan
**Victims & Villains** — Intriguing Sherlockiana from Derham Groves
**Evidence in Blue** — 1938 mystery by E. Charles Vivian
**The Case of the Little Green Men** — Mack Reynolds wrote this love song to sci-fi fans back in 1951 and it's now back in print.
**Hell Fire** — A new hard-boiled novel by Jack Moskovitz about an arsonist, an arson cop and a Nazi hooker. It isn't pretty.
**Researching American-Made Toy Soldiers** — A 276-page collection of a lifetime of articles by toy soldier expert Richard O'Brien
**Strands of the Web: Short Stories of Harry Stephen Keeler** — Edited and Introduced by Fred Cleaver
**The Sam McCain Novels** — Ed Gorman's terrific series includes *The Day the Music Died*, *Wake Up Little Susie* and *Will You Still Love Me Tomorrow?*
**A Shot Rang Out** — Three decades of reviews from Jon Breen
**Mysterious Martin, the Master of Murder** — Two versions of a strange 1912 novel by Tod Robbins about a man who writes books that can kill.
**Dago Red** — 22 tales of dark suspense by Bill Pronzini
**The Night Remembers** — A 1991 Jack Walsh mystery from Ed Gorman
**Rough Cut & New, Improved Murder** — Ed Gorman's first two novels
**Hollywood Dreams** — A novel of the Depression by Richard O'Brien
**Seven Gelett Burgess Novels** — *The Master of Mysteries*, *The White Cat*, *Two O'Clock Courage*, *Ladies in Boxes*, *Find the Woman*, *The Heart Line*, *The Picaroons*
**The Organ Reader** — A huge compilation of just about everything published in the 1971-1972 radical bay-area newspaper, *THE ORGAN*.
**A Clear Path to Cross** — Sharon Knowles short mystery stories by Ed Lynskey
**Old Times' Sake** — Short stories by James Reasoner from Mike Shayne Magazine
**Freaks and Fantasies** — Eerie tales by Tod Robbins, collaborator of Tod Browning on the film FREAKS.
**Six Jim Harmon Double Novels** — *Vixen Hollow/Celluloid Scandal*, *The Man Who Made Maniacs/Silent Siren*, *Ape Rape/Wanton Witch*, *Sex Burns Like Fire/Twist Session*, *Sudden Lust/Passion Strip*, *Sin Unlimited/Harlot Master*, *Twilight Girls/Sex Institution*. Written in the early 60s.
**Marblehead: A Novel of H.P. Lovecraft** — A long-lost masterpiece from Richard A. Lupoff. Published for the first time!
**The Compleat Ova Hamlet** — Parodies of SF authors by Richard A. Lupoff – A brand new edition with more stories and more illustrations by Trina Robbins.
**The Secret Adventures of Sherlock Holmes** — Three Sherlockian pastiches by the Brooklyn author/publisher, Gary Lovisi.
**The Universal Holmes** — Richard A. Lupoff's 2007 collection of five Holmesian pastiches and a recipe for giant rat stew.
**Four Joel Townsley Rogers Novels** — By the author of *The Red Right Hand: Once In a Red Moon*, *Lady With the Dice*, *The Stopped Clock*, *Never Leave My Bed*
**Two Joel Townsley Rogers Story Collections** — Night of Horror and Killing Time
**Twenty Norman Berrow Novels** — *The Bishop's Sword*, *Ghost House*, *Don't Go Out After Dark*, *Claws of the Cougar*, *The Smokers of Hashish*, *The Secret Dancer*, *Don't Jump Mr. Boland!*, *The Footprints of Satan*, *Fingers for Ransom*, *The Three Tiers of Fantasy*, *The Spaniard's Thumb*, *The Eleventh Plague*, *Words Have Wings*, *One Thrilling Night*, *The Lady's in Danger*, *It Howls at Night*, *The Terror in the Fog*, *Oil Under the Window*, *Murder in the Melody*, *The Singing Room*
**The N. R. De Mexico Novels** — Robert Bragg presents *Marijuana Girl*, *Madman on a Drum*, *Private Chauffeur* in one volume.
**Four Chelsea Quinn Yarbro Novels featuring Charlie Moon** — *Ogilvie, Tallant and Moon*, *Music When the Sweet Voice Dies*, *Poisonous Fruit* and *Dead Mice*
**Five Walter S. Masterman Mysteries** — *The Green Toad*, *The Flying Beast*, *The Yellow Mistletoe*, *The Wrong Verdict* and *The Perjured Alibi*. Fantastic impossible plots.
**Two Hake Talbot Novels** — *Rim of the Pit*, *The Hangman's Handyman*. Classic locked room mysteries.
**Two Alexander Laing Novels** — *The Motives of Nicholas Holtz* and *Dr. Scarlett*, stories of medical mayhem and intrigue from the 30s.

**The Werewolf vs the Vampire Woman** — Hard to believe ultraviolence by either Arthur M. Scarm or Arthur M. Scram.

**Black Hogan Strikes Again** — Australia's Peter Renwick pens a tale of the outback.

**Don Diablo: Book of a Lost Film** — Two-volume treatment of a western by Paul Landres, with diagrams. Intro by Francis M. Nevins.

**The Charlie Chaplin Murder Mystery** — Movie hijinks by Wes D. Gehring

**The Koky Comics** — A collection of all of the 1978-1981 Sunday and daily comic strips by Richard O'Brien and Mort Gerberg, in two volumes.

**Suzy** — Another collection of comic strips from Richard O'Brien and Bob Vojtko.

**Dime Novels: Ramble House's 10-Cent Books** — *Knife in the Dark* by Robert Leslie Bellem, *Hot Lead* and *Song of Death* by Ed Earl Repp, *A Hashish House in New York* by H.H. Kane, and five more.

**Blood in a Snap** — The *Finnegan's Wake* of the 21$^{st}$ century, by Jim Weiler

**Stakeout on Millennium Drive** — Award-winning Indianapolis Noir — Ian Woollen.

**Dope Tales #1** — Two dope-riddled classics; *Dope Runners* by Gerald Grantham and *Death Takes the Joystick* by Phillip Condé.

**Dope Tales #2** — Two more narco-classics; *The Invisible Hand* by Rex Dark and *The Smokers of Hashish* by Norman Berrow.

**Dope Tales #3** — Two enchanting novels of opium by the master, Sax Rohmer. *Dope* and *The Yellow Claw.*

**Tenebrae** — Ernest G. Henham's 1898 horror tale brought back.

**The Singular Problem of the Stygian House-Boat** — Two classic tales by John Kendrick Bangs about the denizens of Hades.

**Tiresias** — Psychotic modern horror novel by Jonathan M. Sweet.

**The One After Snelling** — Kickass modern noir from Richard O'Brien.

**The Sign of the Scorpion** — 1935 Edmund Snell tale of oriental evil.

**The House of the Vampire** — 1907 poetic thriller by George S. Viereck.

**An Angel in the Street** — Modern hardboiled noir by Peter Genovese.

**The Devil's Mistress** — Scottish gothic tale by J. W. Brodie-Innes.

**The Lord of Terror** — 1925 mystery with master-criminal, Fantômas.

**The Lady of the Terraces** — 1925 adventure by E. Charles Vivian.

**My Deadly Angel** — 1955 Cold War drama by John Chelton

**Prose Bowl** — Futuristic satire — Bill Pronzini & Barry N. Malzberg .

**Satan's Den Exposed** — True crime in Truth or Consequences New Mexico — Award-winning journalism by the *Desert Journal.*

**The Amorous Intrigues & Adventures of Aaron Burr** — by Anonymous — Hot historical action.

**I Stole $16,000,000** — A true story by cracksman Herbert E. Wilson.

**The Black Dark Murders** — Vintage 50s college murder yarn by Milt Ozaki, writing as Robert O. Saber.

**Sex Slave** — Potboiler of lust in the days of Cleopatra — Dion Leclerq.

**You'll Die Laughing** — Bruce Elliott's 1945 novel of murder at a practical joker's English countryside manor.

**The Private Journal & Diary of John H. Surratt** — The memoirs of the man who conspired to assassinate President Lincoln.

**Dead Man Talks Too Much** — Hollywood boozer by Weed Dickenson

**Red Light** — History of legal prostitution in Shreveport Louisiana by Eric Brock. Includes wonderful photos of the houses and the ladies.

**A Snark Selection** — Lewis Carroll's *The Hunting of the Snark* with two Snarkian chapters by Harry Stephen Keeler — Illustrated by Gavin L. O'Keefe.

**Ripped from the Headlines!** — The Jack the Ripper story as told in the newspaper articles in the *New York* and *London Times.*

**Geronimo** — S. M. Barrett's 1905 autobiography of a noble American.

**The White Peril in the Far East** — Sidney Lewis Gulick's 1905 indictment of the West and assurance that Japan would never attack the U.S.

**The Compleat Calhoon** — All of Fender Tucker's works: Includes *Totah Six-Pack, Weed, Women and Song* and *Tales from the Tower,* plus a CD of all of his songs.

**Totah Six-Pack** — Just Fender Tucker's six tales about Farmington in one sleek volume.

## RAMBLE HOUSE
Fender Tucker, Prop.
www.ramblehouse.com   fender@ramblehouse.com
228-826-1783   10329 Sheephead Drive, Vancleave MS 39565

www.ingramcontent.com/pod-product-compliance
Lightning Source LLC
Chambersburg PA
CBHW030332020726
47493CB00004B/1253